The Creatures on the Bathroom Ceiling

Derek Rose

ORIGINAL WRITING

© 2013 Derek Rose

Art work by Eric Pineda
www.playkill.com

ISBNS
PARENT : 978-1-78237-294-3
EPUB: 978-1-78237-295-0
MOBI: 978-1-78237-296-7
PDF: 978-1-78237-297-4

A CIP catalogue for this book is available from the National Library.

Published by ORIGINAL WRITING LTD., Dublin, 2013.

Printed by CLONDALKIN GROUP, Glasnevin, Dublin 11

Acknowledgements

I need to thank the following people for their support, professionalism and friendship.

Nicole Hodson for her incredible attention to detail regarding the edit and guidance from start to finish with every aspect of the story. Eric Pineda for his beautiful cover artwork and Denise O'Kelly Literary Editor, for her craft and friendship.

My family and Sophie Lamarque wink wink!

CONTENTS

Chapter One

AN INTRODUCTION

Francis Williams lived with both his parents and younger sister, Alex, at number 46 North Great George's Street on the north side of the River Liffey in Dublin. Their father was an archaeologist, he named his daughter Alex, short for Alexandria, after the great library founded in ancient Egypt. Their mother had named Francis after a saint, with him being born on the feast day March 12th. After the birth of her second child, she had become a housewife, giving up her daytime job to look after her children as she couldn't stand to see how her first child smiled with outstretched arms at the crèche staff every morning.

Although from outward appearances everything looked normal, Francis was slightly different from other teenagers. That's just the way it was. He did all the normal things an eighteen-year-old boy would do: chased girls, bunked off school and generally just enjoyed himself having a laugh with his friends. But he still felt different because he wanted more. The problem was that he had no understanding of what and how much, and, regrettably, this led him to misunderstand many situations in normal everyday life. On the upside, he was a very talented young artist and wished to enter a prestige art college if he was offered a place. Francis loved to paint on anything; a fact not gone unnoticed by his teachers. At a young age, he felt passionate about almost everything. He fell in love with anything other than reality and slowly lost touch with the real world, preferring to enjoy the dreams of his mind where everything was possible and subsequently had started searching for passion in the real world.

As for school, he was just an average boy, nothing special. However, the balance of power between his heart and mind had marked him as unique. Discovering love for his parents, the colour orange, anything green, Hanna-Barbera the creators of the *Tom and Jerry* cartoons and knowing that he was just a creature standing on a rock floating helplessly through space at sixty thousand miles an hour woke him up. Funny as it may seem, looking back he never thought he could have been so happy, having more friends at school than he could count. Ever since Alex and he had received the magical candle from the old woman at the corner shop, the direction of their lives had been changed forever.

Stranger still, the corner shop from which they got the candle never seemed to be open when they wanted to enter, but only when they didn't. So you can understand how difficult it was to return to the shop. Every night since they received the candle Francis had pretended to take a bath as a cover story to his parents. "We just couldn't stop" he used to repeat to himself all day long pretending to be in the middle of some television or radio interview about his amazing discoveries as an explorer. It's something most teenagers would never have looked forward to, the bath that is. But Francis, of course, wasn't actually taking a bath, just getting exactly what he wanted on the bathroom ceiling. It was similar to a drip you see attached to the arm of patient in hospital: feeding them slowly with just enough to survive. Those little drops sucked Francis in like a hunger for meat you can be crazy for.

If Francis had understood then what he was getting himself into, and known where it might finish, would he have continued? Well, the answer is yes, as the final outcome was always going to be a little uncertain because of the element of chance. He had always taken chances because you never know what's around the next turn. Knowing nothing of how his journey would develop, the rest would be all down to him alone. In fact, where Alex and he both ended up resembled a fantasy novel! A truly, fabulous, magical place, swelling with so much contentment . . . or so he thought at the outset. It was like being offered the winning prize ticket for some grand competition you had forgotten you even entered. Making it possibly the best moment in his short life to date. Something this fantastic and amazing nobody would ever have believed Francis and Alex until the day they both vanished in the bathroom steam.

It was a Friday in late June 2010 and Francis was just about to turn eighteen. He wanted to have the party tonight but his mum had said it was bad luck. "You need to have the party on your birthday" she had repeated numerous times. This kind of drained his mood somewhat, as a few close friends were unable to attend on Saturday. Thankfully Alex was still excited at the prospect of a party the next day which helped cheer him up a little. She was a very special sister in ways Francis found hard to understand sometimes. The fact she could predict who was about to enter a room from behind a closed door or answer a question before it was asked was enough. After school that day, both of them were dragged off for a walk along the beach with their mum and her friend. Being eighteen and bumping into one of the most beautiful girls in school with your mother, her friend and your sister could only end in embarrassment. Her name was Ann Marie and she was simply stunning. For most of the boys in his year, she was the hot topic whenever she passed by in the corridor. The type of girl everyone wanted to hang out with because everyone said she was so nice. He'd chatted to her once or twice but it was always regarding school. Other than that, he knew absolutely nothing about her except that all the guys drooled over her.

Now here she was, alone on the beach walking straight towards them. Francis being a few feet ahead of the others quickly realised he would reach her first. He looked around pretending to be interested in the water but no matter what he did his gaze returned to her. There was a lack of competition on the beach unlike in the schoolyard. She approached looking down at the sand a number of times and just when Francis was about to open his mouth he heard.

"Hi Ann Marie, how's your mother keeping? Well, I hope." His mum shouted from behind. He didn't even turn around as a voice from inside his head was screaming, *Stop! PLEASE shut up Mum, God!* But judging from Ann Marie's smiling face she knew his mother.

"Oh hi, Mrs Williams. She's well, thanks," she shouted back.

Then it happened. Ann Marie had reached the top of his shadow on the sand when she tripped sideways. Quickly righting herself, she fell again forward, came up and stumbled into him. It was a movie; two huge oil tankers meeting on the high seas, their hulls smashing in slow motion. One ship ripping into the port side of the other, crushing its steel and entangling the railings. Then after the impact pushing one another these great giants separated as the monstrous waves swelled up around their hulls. He did catch her but in the worst possible way.

His head fell directly onto her shoulder with his face touching her neck for a single second. But that was enough. His nose did the rest, sucking in all his senses would allow. As they came apart again Francis found he couldn't speak. Still trying to work out the information overload he had just received. He imagined his brain didn't have enough ram and had crashed. Her smell was just so clean, he thought. The awkwardness lasted only a moment, as Ann Marie quickly started to chat.

"Thanks for that," she said grinning, which helped immensely.

"Francis, did you invite Ann Marie to your birthday party?" his mother asked.

"Ah no, never got the chance Mum," he answered embarrassed, after a short pause and stared his mother straight in the eyes.

"If you're doing nothing tomorrow night, sure come along," he urged.

"Yeah, I'd love to come to the party. Can I bring some friends?"

"Of course."

After everything was sorted they said goodbye and parted. But something was different. By eighteen, Francis had had a few girlfriends, short romances but this was strange as he didn't bother to look back at Ann Marie. This made him think as they continued walking.

At the end of the beach they rested on a large, flat outcrop of stone, which must have been here since time began. It looked so solid and strong. Tapping it with his finger he wondered what fantastic sights it must have seen over the thousands of years it had stood here.

"Bet you have some great stories," he said firmly, but no answer came, of course.

Francis's mother was busy chatting about house prices and such with her friend, so he watched his sister's head ticking from side to side like a pendulum as she marched up and down over the huge stretch of broken shell and stones. It looked a little strange, almost comical, seeing her movements. She was a machine scanning the ground when abruptly she stopped, frozen as if she had lost something and then started to dig. What's she up to now, he thought, glancing to heaven. She had found something and came running. "Francis, this is definitely for you," she explained opening her hand.

"Nice piece."

"Don't pretend Francis, I know you like it."

He took a proper look. Francis had seen thousands of stones collected by his father over the years and knew it by the name rhodonite. Sort of light grey to brown with criss-crossing lines of black, orange and red with a mix of different shades of pink running through it.

"It's beautiful, no shit," nodding his head in agreement.

"It called to me, begging to be picked up," she said excitedly.

"You mean of all the rocks, stones and pebbles on this beach this one called to you. Jumped up, slapped you in the face screaming save me from this life of hell Pleeeeeeeeaassse!"

"Yes, sort of," Alex stated looking very serious. Francis tossed it into the air. Catching it again he brought up his arm hoping to return it into the sea, when she shouted.

"Don't, please Francis. Put it in your pocket. It's going to bring you luck."

Francis hadn't seen Alex so worked up in ages as he rubbed the stone between his fingers, which for some strange reason was very relaxing and beautiful to the touch which made him smile.

Chapter Two

THE OLD LADY'S SHOP

Enough had happened already in the day that Francis was ready to lounge on the couch watching his favourite television shows but the weirdest encounter was still to happen at the bottom of their street. Their mother's friend had left them some time back so it was just the three of them rounding the corner at the bottom of North Great George's Street. The surrounding area had become rundown over the last sixty years, but the fact that James Joyce had lived on the street for a time always assured a measure of importance to the city regarding tourism. Georgian homes of the long-dead rich were now rented out as apartments to students and families.

"Wait a moment," their mum said, with a curious expression on her face. "I didn't see that before."

"It's a new shop, let's take a look," Alex suggested while pulling Francis towards the door.

"Never noticed it before either," Francis said looking at the sign above the shop which read *Odds and Ends*. Their mum took one look inside.

"It's full of junk," she continued, "you two can have a look round but don't stay long. Dinner is in fifteen minutes," she said in a raised voice hurrying off. As Francis and Alex approached the shop door their mum was looking back towards them both pointing her finger at her watch. Making sure they understood not to be late again.

"Alex, slow down, it's not going anywhere," Francis shouted, as he was dragged through the shop door. When he passed over the threshold of the door, a wind blew out from inside the shop. It felt as if he was being cleaned by some invisible force which raised the hairs on the back of his neck. He felt uneasy.

"Alex, slow down," he said nervously. Francis looked around hoping to see another customer browsing the shelves. Nobody. It was very quiet and a little unsettling as the lighting was so poor in places.

"Hello," he announced. No answer came so he walked in a little further past the first row of shelves hoping to spot the shopkeeper.

"Hello," Francis repeated a little louder. Again nothing. Must be out back, he thought.

The place may have been badly kept, but it was full of incredible stuff. Francis simply couldn't resist looking round. There were jugs the size of Alex, painted in colours you couldn't put a name to. Strange material of every description was hanging from the roof. The shelf next to the entrance was full of toys made of tin: sailors, soldiers, tanks and planes but not the same as they make them today. They had real faces, expressions of pain and fear, kind of creepy.

Alex was out of sight when she yelped, "Francis, come quickly!" It took a moment for him to reach her, which only added to his surprise. She was standing there looking at a small, golden carousel spinning around. It was both wonderful and weird. The very same reflecting balls you see hanging from the roof of a disco with beams of light filling the room.

"Stop, Alex, you're going to hypnotise yourself," he cautioned.

"I'm controlling it. God, I love this place," she laughed.

"What are you talking about, controlling it?" Francis asked nervously looking around expecting someone to jump out.

You're doing a great job at controlling the carousel Alex, don't stop. I must admit you're extremely talented for someone so young replied a soft voice inside her head.

"Thank you. I love your shop," Alex replied

"Sorry what, Alex? Who are you talking to?" Francis asked. Oh she's chatting to me a voice said inside Francis's head. "Jesus Christ!" Screaming, Francis fell back knocking over everything from the shelf behind him. *Sorry I didn't mean to frighten you* came the voice again.

"What, what, who are you? No, where are you?" as he looked around terrified.

"Alex did you hear that?" he stuttered.

"Yes, it's strange but kind of funny, don't you think? I've been chatting to Eloïse for a few minutes now. She's really nice, it's her shop."

Oh Alex please don't overdo it came the voice again. Francis raised both his hands covering his ears.

"Please stop doing that," he shouted. "This woman is inside my head, Alex, talking to me without the use of my ears."

Alex took Francis by the hand to try and reassure him everything was ok. She sensed her brother needed to relax, as he was completely unprepared for this nightmare. The beams of light slowly disappeared once the spinning carousel came to a stop. Feeling more relaxed, he closed his eyes and in the blackness exhaled long and slow.

"Alex, what the hell is going on? How did she do that and who is this woman?" he asked.

"It's called telepathy, I think," she said.

"I know what it's called but that woman really did it. Wait a moment!" Francis looked about a little on edge again. "Ok if it's not a trick then what the hell is she, a bloody witch?" he added with a sarcastic tone in an attempt to belittle her words.

Alex stood there with a shocked expression on her face. Francis was unaware the woman was now standing directly behind him.

"A witch! A witch!" came a scream from the woman.

Francis leapt with fright.

"A witch. Well I never, what an insult. I've been called a lot of names over the years, but a WITCH." She was now running off towards the front of the shop holding her heavy dress up above her feet ranting. This old lady could move. "Anything but that," she continued.

Realising Francis may have overstepped the mark, Alex ran after her followed quickly by her brother who was completely overwhelmed with indecision.

"What! I didn't pop into someone's mind without permission and start talking to them," he said to himself feeling a little guilty. Eloïse was now standing behind the counter banging it with her fists. She was looking at both of them. Her eyes stretched wide open.

"I went to university for two hundred years," she boasted, followed by complete silence.

Both of them were too afraid to talk, so stood there and stared at her. After a while she realised her ranting was having the opposite effect. Every time she slammed down with her fist her long black hair rocked forward over her face. She could have been a drummer in some Seventies rock band. Both of them started laughing. Thankfully, the old woman saw it also and joined in. It was absolutely hysterical. Everyone was now laughing. Eloïse started weeping it was so funny; the tears come flowing down her face. As Eloïse wiped her eyes, her hands quickly became very wet and the tears kept coming. She took a towel from the back of the door and within a few moments it was totally soaked.

"This is nuts," Francis admitted. How could so much water come from a little old lady?

Looking to Alex, she shook her head in disbelief also as it kept on coming. The counter top was now flooded and the laughter had stopped, but it was still flowing everywhere.

"Are you ok?" Alex cried out with deep concern. It could have been a couple of litres by now.

"Help me look for some towels, quickly, Alex," Francis snapped.

She was fixated on the water flowing from Eloïse, which now covered most of the shop floor. This was serious; the old lady looked in real pain.

"What can we do?" Francis shouted.

"Nothing, it will pass," Eloïse groaned.

Alex had found some cleaning towels and was busy mopping up the water. Francis had totally forgotten that he had some tissues in his pocket. He quickly realised one packet of tissues would be useless but he wanted to help. Immediately he reached into his trousers pocket and in one handful grabbed everything. Holding out his arm he slowly opened his palm to reveal some coins, a bus ticket, chewing gum, the tissues and the small stone Alex had given him at the beach. Suddenly feeling so useless he shook his head and was about to return the contents to his pocket when Eloïse started chanting. The stone began twitching in his palm, forcing him to toss everything on the counter top.

"What is it?" he asked frantically.

The old lady looked surprised. The water had slowed to a mere trickle and although she was taking large breaths she showed signs of recovering from whatever madness they had witnessed. The stone on the other hand was still moving. It rolled about, and nearly fell off the counter twice.

"Nobody move," she snapped, repeating more sinisterly, "nobody move."

By the sound of her voice she was deadly serious. Francis and Alex stood motionless watching as the stone rolled about. Eloïse sounded as if she was chanting something under her breath in a strange language. Suddenly the stone starting spinning faster and faster like a coin goes whirling around on a flat surface. But they always lose their energy and eventually come to a stop, as the stone did. Unfortunately, it wasn't over as the stone appeared to be absorbing the water from the counter top. Both Francis and Alex took a step backwards as they looked on in disbelief. The stone had started to expand in size. The tears from Eloïse seemed to be acting as some sort of powerhouse to be fed on. In moments, the thing was the size of a football.

"I don't like the look of this Francis," Alex said nervously.

"Know what you mean," he replied.

Eloïse was in a trance, her eyes fixated on the stone that was now larger than the cash register and still growing. As a mist formed in the room, nearly all the water in the shop had been absorbed by the stone. Even the water on the floor had started to evaporate and was being sucked towards it. The stone was now so big that the counter was beginning to break under its weight. Alex reached out to grab Francis's hand. Eloïse was still ranting, but Francis was no longer listening. He was staring at this growing stone. Starry lights flashed across its beautiful surface, something Francis had failed to notice before. It was like seeing a baby in a mother's womb. The criss-crossing lines of orange and pink were veins pumping blood through some unnatural creature. Suddenly Francis saw a shape inside. Squinting his eyes, he leaned forward a little.

"Oh my God," he said softly.

It wasn't a creature. It was a girl staring directly at him. His upper body jolted like that first time you taste whiskey straight. She must have been made of porcelain. Francis couldn't resist, but he had to. Reaching out, he touched the stone and in return he received pain, agonising pain, ripping through his body he instantly knew it stole something from him right there and then. But he didn't seem to mind; in fact, he was happy to give it up. So he touched it again and the expression he saw on her peaceful face made his stomach pull in and the hairs on his neck started twitching.

Having no idea what was happening, Francis stood motionless looking straight at her when out of the blue there was a flash of light and he collapsed on the ground. Moments later Eloïse was whispering, "Its fine, your sister is safe and so are you." Opening his eyes to discover that he was lying on the floor with Eloïse and Alex kneeling over him was a bit of a shock. Eloïse took a small wood chipping from inside the dress she was wearing. "Sniff once," she suggested.

"What happened?" he answered drowsily.

"Something truly amazing," Eloïse said with a smile. "I never thought that today was going to be so exciting, I love you two."

"But you were in pain," Alex stressed. Because she had been very concerned.

"No, no, no, I was living a dream, a dream I haven't lived, in an age of time you cannot measure upon this world," she paused, seeming so content with the utter happiness in her old face. Sitting up Francis listened as Eloïse started to explain what had happened. "Whatever you may learn in school Francis and

Alex," looking straight at both of them, "all life didn't start on earth!"

"There's ALIENS!" screamed Alex.

Eloïse smiled, paused a moment and then continued. "This universe is far too huge and exquisite," she explained tossing her arms into the air.

Alex had now sat down beside her brother listening intently. "All I know is that this little gem you found was there at the beginning of a phase of life."

"You mean the big bang thing?" Alex interrupted again.

"No, that's far too old, nobody knows what was going on then, except Sandstone maybe!"

"Sandstone?" Alex asked looking to Francis. Eloïse ignored Alex, continuing regardless.

"I'm talking about two hundred thousand years ago maybe! When life, birth, death whatever you want to call it happened, this little thing was present." She held up the small gem stone right in front of their faces and again she repeated with such a youthful smile. "This little gem was present at the beginning, the very start."

"Whoa?" Alex cried with excitement.

Francis was listening to what Eloïse had said, but couldn't stop thinking about that face he had seen and what he had felt. His parents knew he was a total dreamer and very passionate about drawing and would probably go to art college. He loved life and even then realised that he couldn't survive without passion. Touching the stone, if only for a moment, was like finding a doorway to endless passion, something of which he had no understanding yet wanted more. As Eloïse helped Francis to his feet, Alex nudged him.

"We better be going, Mum will do her nut if we are late for dinner again!"

"Before you both go, I have something for you, and it's very important that you listen to what I have to say!" Eloïse went through the door behind the counter and started tossing boxes about while shouting. "Where are you? I know you're in here."

Francis and Alex just shrugged their shoulders wondering what she was up to.

"YES!" came a scream from the back room. Eloïse then promptly returned with an old wooden box, which she gently laid down on the counter top.

"Firstly, Francis. Please take back your stone as you will need it."

"Yeah but will it be staying the same size?" he asked nervously.

"Yes, it will," she replied calmly, laughing.

Opening the box very carefully all three of them peaked inside to see some very fine cloth wrapping an object. Eloïse lifted the object from the box and unwrapped it in such a manner that whatever lay within could only be of great value.

"This candle wasn't made, it was grown," she said.

Approximately six inches long divided into sections of different colours. Starting at the top with red, then orange, next blue, then red again, green, last being black.

"Once you light the candle Francis, a connection a bridge will start to form to somewhere you have been waiting to see," Eloïse continued, "each colour represents a different world. Once lit and the other world is fully formed around you blow it out and you will be transported to that world. To return simply relight the candle and do the same once you're home.

"Where are these worlds, Eloïse?" Alex marvelled.

Eloïse again ignored Alex with a smile, "its part of the spell, my dear, but you best remember once the colour is gone you can never return to that world. NEVER. So don't get yourselves stuck there!"

"Then why is the colour red marked twice on the candle?" Francis asked.

Eloïse was in deep thought for a moment nodding her head.

"Don't know, must be a mistake I made . . . why is that?" she asked herself. Eloïse looked puzzled for a moment.

"And what do you want us to do with it?" Francis questioned.

"Use it and see what happens, the rest will look after itself," she replied.

Knowing their mother was expecting them, Francis and Alex were already running for the door.

"Bring the stone with you, Francis, when you use the candle!" Eloïse shouted from behind.

Chapter Three

THE BEGINNING

Immediately after dinner, Francis and his sister ran to his room.

"Give me the lighter," he ordered seriously.

"No, I want to do it," she snapped, putting her hands behind her back.

"Look we're going to do this together so let me try it first and then we can take turns."

"NO. We should toss for it," she pleaded.

"God. OK. Heads you lose, tails I win. OK!"

"Do I not get a choice?" She glared at him.

"Forget the toss then, Alex. You start," and slowly a smile appeared on her face.

He took a deep breath and ripped the fine cloth from around the candle. Precisely at that moment, he realised he would never look at a candle in the same way ever again, no matter what transpired, possessed as he was by what was happening right now in this very moment of his life. What a day, he thought. Meeting a real witch, seeing a beautiful girl inside a stone that his sister found on the beach, and then being told to go on some crazy adventure. While the thought lingered in his head, Alex pushed her thumb down on the lighter cog to connect the flint and ignite the gas. It seemed an eternity as she moved the lighter towards the wick.

"Go on," he said.

Once the wick warmed up, it started to make a crackling noise, tiny sparks splashing outward and disappearing into thin air then suddenly it was lit. Both of them looked around not knowing what to expect. There wasn't a sound in the room except for the muffled noises from the television downstairs.

They were sitting approximately four feet away from the candle as it flickered. It was so weird; the rest of the room appeared dark with just a few metres of light surrounding the candle, even though the light was switched on. They were inside a ball of light, but somehow relaxing, probably to calm the nerves of the traveller, Francis thought.

After five minutes passed, they wondered if anything was going to happen. They both had their own ideas as to how it would actually begin but that's not how it started. "Do you hear that Francis, the wind blowing through the trees or over some great ocean."

"No, its waves breaking on a beach," he answered.

It was amazing. Somehow the ceiling started to move like ripples on a pond after you toss some small pebbles in. It was even bending the top of the doorframe. In an instant, everything was interrupted by the noise of their mother charging up the stairs.

"Alex! Francis! Your turn for the dishes and NO excuses. Your father is really tired."

She paused a moment on the landing waiting for a reply, then started shouting, "Well I'M not doing them again!"

"Quick, blow it out, Alex!"

Dread and panic hit them both. With one breath it was all gone and everything in the room returned to normal as their mother came charging through the door.

"Move it! Come on!" She paused looking towards the smoking candle.

"What are you two doing?" she demanded.

"Ahhh, it's a candle," Francis said, while trying not to sound sarcastic

"I can see that, Francis. What are you doing with it lit in your bedroom? You know how dangerous they can be!"

"Well it's an . . . you know, an insane candle," he replied. Alex looked to Francis followed by his mother, who was beginning to laugh also.

"An insane candle," his mother said as she folded her arms looking to him as only mothers can.

"Insane. Did I say insane?"

Alex nodded, her head gleaming.

"Ahhh yes. I meant incense yes incense, which I bought for Alex from Eloïse, I mean the old lady in that shop down the street."

Surprisingly his mother loved it, saying how nice it was of him. She came over and rubbed her hand over his hair.

"That is so sweet of you, Francis. You are turning into a very kind young man."

"Did he really do that?" she asked Alex.

Alex peered up at her mother with an open mouth and gradually the word "yes" passed over her lips.

"Great, but you're still washing the dishes!" their mother repeated.

Later that night, Francis and Alex discussed how they were going to get away with this. Honestly they didn't care, both wanting to light the candle right there and then though thankfully they came up with a better plan. Francis would fill the bath every night this week and pretend to be having a relaxing wash.

"No, that won't work; she'll catch us for sure," he said.

"Yeah you're right, she comes upstairs to check you turned off the hot water tank after you get into the bath, and for any other reasons. If our bedroom doors are closed early she will knock and come in to see all is good," she added with a depressed tone.

He pushes his hand deep into his pocket and grasped the stone.

"You know what? It doesn't matter. Let's go with the flow."

Sometime after ten that night, alone in his room Francis was still holding the stone as he lay in bed. He kept on imagining over and over how large it had been in the shop today. His heart was racing, in what direction he had no idea, but he was sure the stone was responsible. He possessed a truly remarkable memory. Ever since he could remember he had the ability while lying in bed drifting off to sleep at night, to recall visions of the past day to study in better detail -- his private time he called it -- but tonight for the first time he was holding all that he needed in his hand. After all that had occurred today, he should be in a straight jacket, doped up by some lovely nurse in a psychiatric ward!

The lamp beside the bed provided enough light for him to see the stone, his mind did the rest. Rubbing its soft surface only added to the confusion. Was something, somebody really inside, he thought? He took a deep breath. Was he falling in love with a stone?!?! He started laughing to himself. Really? A stone that my sister gave me? Not that Francis understood all of what love was but he knew what letting somebody into your life is, and then suddenly they are gone.

Taking chances was what he did well, why change now? "There's plenty of fish in the sea," Mum always said. Placing the stone to his forehead, its cool surface felt warm and cold at the same time. Remembering the girl's eyes from when he saw her in the shop today, his mind created an image of a lighthouse beacon drawing him towards her. He imagined being a ship in the ocean with the light from her eyes leading him to his doom, the exact opposite of what a lighthouse is intended for. He smiled as his mind put their first encounter into more normal situations. Maybe she was standing at the counter in some pub buying a drink the very same day he was legally allowed inside to buy a drink and he asked her a question, she replied and that was it: the spark instantly became a fire, for the deep scorching inferno of a relationship to follow.

As he was drifting off to sleep his last thoughts were of himself gliding on some great ocean far from land; hearing the distant thunder only added to the reality of his dreams, that night, and the greatest nightmare Francis Williams would ever freely walk into.

Chapter Four

STRANGE DAYS

Waking up the next morning was like nothing Francis had ever experienced. His sister was jumping up and down at the bottom of his bed causing him to rock violently on this rough sea he was still dreaming about when awkwardly he was tossed from the raft of broken wood and landed on a pebble beach. Opening his eyes was easy, but the pain was hard. Something was very wrong. His head was pounding and he was covered in sweat. At first he thought it felt like a hangover but he hadn't experienced too many of them in his short life so far. Pulling back the covers to hear his sister shouting "Happy Birthday!" he tried smiling but at the same time noticed something hard digging into his back. Remembering the stone, he reached down and pulled it from under the covers hiding it from Alex. Now sitting up, Francis put his other hand to his head.

"Jesus, what's happening with me?" he groaned.

"It's your birthday. You are eighteen today, Francis!" she shouted.

"Thanks, but no thanks," and ducked his head under the covers. Alex yanked hard on the covers.

"You can do whatever you want! ANYTHING! Stay out all night, leave the country, have sex. Anyway mum made you a special breakfast, so you better get up. Ok?" she said and ran off.

Francis didn't dare tell Alex what was going on as he wasn't sure himself but it felt like he had lived a dream the previous night. Like he was awake and walking around in it. Every part of his body was aching, especially his head. Looking at the stone now in clear daylight and after all the events of yesterday, he felt a swelling of an unidentified emotion. The stone looked even nicer, its red and orange veins appeared even more human-like or so he thought. He was still staring at the stone when his mother's shouting made him leap from his bed.

After breakfast, his mother and father started preparing the house for his birthday party. Francis had asked about twenty or so friends, mostly guys but they were bringing a few girls too, hoping to make it a good healthy mix. Alex had also asked some of her friends, as their mother said it was fair. There would be a good few parents as well, nice excuse for their father to chill out with some mates; he had the greatest music collection around and insisted on being DJ.

Around six, Francis had a serious discussion with Alex regarding Eloïse, the stone and everything that had happened in the past two days. She would say nothing and that was that. Then the first group of friends started arriving. Gradually, within two hours the kitchen and living room were totally full of people.

For the most part the party was really cool. Their father played his usual party tricks and their mother dished out food. Francis looked happy, but like Alex lighting the candle was the only thing on his mind, which would have to wait until tomorrow regardless of how much it dulled both their moods. As promised, Ann Marie had come to the party, which delighted Francis but being pushed into a position with a beautiful girl in whom suddenly he had no interest, frightened Francis. When he approached offering some cocktail sausages, she was standing with some of her friends. Holding his nose high in the air like a French waiter.

"Madam, refreshments," he said in a posh accent.

"Oh, I would love one," she replied smiling, with an even more stuck-up facial response.

They both started laughing and Ann Marie introduced him to her friends. After some moving about with different people passing by on their way to the garden, they found themselves facing each other, once again. She thanked him for the invitation to the party.

Francis found himself nodding, which was strange as he must have seemed really relaxed and not over interested. Normally he would have been trying too hard, he thought. Then a friend cut into their conversation, as friends can, and pointed to the garden.

"See you in a bit," he said.

She nodded cheerfully. As he exited the room something compelled him to glance back. Seeing all her girlfriends' heads come together like vultures over a dead carcass, as girls do, but he didn't care one bit. His friend asked, "How's it going with Ann Marie?"

"Don't know," he shrugged his shoulders.

"What? She's a total hottie," came his friend's shocked response.

"Yeah, I know. Let's see what happens."

They both laughed.

"I'm thinking about someone else," Francis continued as he drank slowly from his glass of beer.

His dad was busy playing the classics like Blondie's "Maria" which most people were dancing to. Being of two left feet, his success was limited but Ann Marie didn't seem to mind. They danced for a while and got separated, but Francis never tried to make his way back. She must have thought he was playing hard to get, but Francis was deep in thought as he realised that this is how a murderer must think. Look at the power I have over her, and realising the lengths we go to in trying to achieve our goals. Ann Marie gave up trying to reach Francis after three attempts. For the first time, a beautiful girl was chasing him and he totally ignored all her advances. Even Alex had noticed. When the time came to say goodbye, he kissed her on the cheek. He knew she wanted more, but it would never happen.

Later that night before bed, Alex kept pestering him to light the candle although they had decided to start on Sunday night as not to arouse suspicion. It was too late anyway. Francis's eyes passed with wonder over the candle's bright red top and below to the black bottom. Something they had failed to notice the first time was that the red coloured section now had very small images carved into its side, suggesting water and a beach.

"That wasn't there before we lit it, was it?" she asked.

"No it's new, maybe it's a way of telling you what kind of world it is?"

"A warning, good or bad," she stressed.

Only after a detailed inspection did Alex agree to let him sleep. Afterwards, saying good night, she took it to her room wrapped in the same fine cloth.

Lying in bed, Francis's thoughts were far from settling. Looking up at his ceiling, which had been moving last night by the means of a magical candle, he couldn't stop thinking of the events which had taken place over the last few days. The image of the girl trapped in this little stone flashed in and out of his mind, as he gently moved it with his fingertips. Over the years, he had seen hundreds of rocks that his father had brought home from every corner of the world. Most were boring browns and greys although he kept a few on the windowsill for a time. But never had he carried one around with him, let alone taken it to bed. Regarding his state of mind, if his friends at school ever found out it would be the nail in the coffin.

Before closing his eyes he took a last peek at the stone. Bringing it to his forehead, rubbing it down the side of his face like glass he imagined how her skin would feel to the touch. Could he actually hear the soft breaking waves of a beach? Fantasizing about the first time he saw her eyes, and naked body, in Eloïse's shop. Luckily, the madness had not reached new heights, so he removed the stone to the side dresser before sleeping.

On Sunday morning, Francis slept until nearly eleven, but he awoke feeling stiff again. Bending his knee to leave the bed he immediately sensed something was not right.

"WHAT?" he shouted.

Pulling back the covers his leg felt really heavy, like wet sand. Limping across the room to the mirror, the stiffness was extremely alarming. There were markings on the lower part of his leg. At first, it resembled slate or graphite. Francis frantically hobbled about the room trying to return his leg to what he considered normal.

"Jesus Christ! What is up with me?" banging his foot on the floor.

After a few moments, the strange feeling subsided. Looking to his side dresser the stone was missing. Yanking the covers off the bed, he discovered the little stone was sitting there.

"That's it," he yelped, imagining himself marching down to the corner shop, kicking open the shop door screaming at her to end this madness. Of course, this never happened because he really didn't want all this to end.

Alex and their mother had gone shopping before lunch and their dad was gardening out the back. Waiting for the moment he could light the candle, Francis watched TV all day; the stone never left his fingers.

When they returned carrying huge shopping bags full of the week's groceries, everyone helped to unpack. Alex had looked to Francis questioningly a few times. Eventually giving in, they made their way upstairs. Behind the closed door in his room, she started talking about the shop being closed as they had passed by. Francis told her he was feeling strange and would also like to talk to Eloïse, but left out the part about his dreams the last two days and the condition of his body each morning.

"Do you remember she said the shop only opens if you don't want to enter?"

"Yes," he replied

"We have to be thinking of something else when we get there," she said grinning.

"Ok, tomorrow before lunch we will try it, but tonight we have to work out some kind of plan for lighting it and not getting caught."

Suddenly Alex's face lit up as she dashed to her room looking to pack supplies for the trip.

Later that evening.

"Mum, I'm going to take a bath," he shouted down the stairs.

"Don't use all the water, Alex can have one after you," she shouted back.

Their house may have been old but all of their mother's friends loved the old French bathtub. It stood alone, away from the wall so you could walk around it. The water pipes came up directly beneath the tub to the taps, which were very ornate. Unlike modern baths the taps were fitted at the centre. After the bath was filled, Francis topped it up with bubble bath for the final effect. He shouted to Alex through the open door. When she arrived he dragged her in.

"Easy there," she insisted with a worried look.

"I don't want to mess this up."

"Francis it's cool. Relax!" she stressed trying to settle him down.

Alex pulled the candle from her bag and lit it crossing the room. Francis's heart was racing as it started to glow. Both of them were looking at the ceiling waiting for something to happen. Steam was now rising from the water, curling until it reached the roof, adding to the wonderment of it all.

"God, it is all so Dali," Alex said while starting to sniff.

"Do you smell that?" he said looking from one corner of the ceiling to the other.

"Yeah, smells like the sea, really fresh," she replied.

Without warning suddenly it got exciting as little flashes of miniature lightning appeared on the ceiling. Followed by dark clouds and for the first time they heard thunder. The best way to describe it was flying in a balloon above the earth. The picture was clear. They could see shapes, a beach and some buildings inland. Becoming so excited, they failed to notice the image had frozen in what looked like a street, from a spaghetti western.

"Francis, the candle," Alex urged. It had already burnt through one third of the red colour at its tip.

"God, it's not giving us much time?" he admitted

Alex pointed to the wall where the image seemed to be flowing down from the ceiling like water and the faster it flowed the more of the other world they saw. Francis judged that in a few moments the whole room would be surrounded by this other world. Blinding flashes of light filled the room forcing them to cover their eyes as the lightning increased putting them both on edge.

What happened next was truly terrifying. A humongous blast like a bomb exploded right over their heads. Alex was thrown to the floor screaming, knocking the candle over as she fell and instantly the other world was gone. The force of the air blast from the other world had passed freely into their bathroom because of the connection and had shook the entire house violently. It was so loud that Francis's eardrums nearly burst. Twenty seconds later, both their parents had charged into the bathroom ranting and raving. Their father was a life saver, he had read somewhere about freak lightning strikes in the tropics, it was such a ridiculous story that Francis even started to believe it himself. Their mother was holding onto Alex while looking around the room. With all the steam it was hard to see the window at the back. She checked Francis over twice before shouting orders to their father who it seemed was unable to stop coming up with strange explanations to what had happened.

Alex was a little shaken but soon enough was laughing. It took only about ten minutes before the police arrived; everyone on the street must have called at the same time. Francis' parents spent half the night chatting with the neighbours about the explosion. After checking on Alex again, he went to bed exhausted and even more attached to this new world than he had ever felt. He should have been thinking about smashing the damn candle in front of Eloïse and screaming to her, "Go get stuffed with your magic, you BITCH! I've had it up to here with this shit!" Knowing that would never happen, he kept rubbing the stone gently through his fingers only to wake each morning feeling he had spent days under the covers with her.

Of course, Francis had never left his bedroom but the power of the stone, and his obsession with her, strengthened their bond every second he held it. Pushing the tiny stone across his forehead over the rim of his dry lips, he imagined lying down beside her happily falling asleep on a beach somewhere. Anywhere, so long he held this, his, little gem.

Chapter Five

THE OTHER PLACE

This particular Monday was the worst ever. Nothing as of yet in his life had gone so slowly. Their mother had decided to clean the entire house from top to bottom and demanded that Francis and Alex assist until at least lunchtime. His mother had handed him cleaning liquids that he couldn't properly pronounce, nor had he heard of before. So, by twelve o'clock, Francis had a desperate expression on his face. All he wanted was to reach Eloïse's shop and subject her to a million questions. Exactly the way you imagine the first interview between a human and an alien would go.

Finally relieved of duty, they both rushed from the house. As they walked along the street, there was no mention of, "Oh see you later, off to my mate's house," from either of them. Bar being arrested, nothing would now stop them from going to the shop. At some distance from the entrance they halted.

"Alex, the plan?" he asked like a private to his officer in the army.

"Think nothing of the shop, nothing," she replied.

"Ok. So I will be thinking of . . . umm . . . something but not the shop." What picture could he hold in his mind, he wondered? It took about a second for him to start smiling as he rubbed the stone in his pocket. He would simply hold her face in his mind.

"Good I have something too," Alex said eagerly

Francis was a little surprised she hadn't revealed what or who she was thinking of. Keeping it to herself was very unlike her, he thought. But they were still walking towards the shop and nothing else really mattered at all except reaching it.

So with these thoughts they walked down the street pulling faces. By the time they reached the shop, both of them had completely forgotten about it. In fact the plan had worked so well; metres away Francis remembered this might actually work.

"Brilliant," he said gleaming with joy. Rounding the corner, they saw that the shop door was locked and the shutter pulled down.

"Jesus Christ, we will never get in. What do we have to do?" he shouted, pushing his hands over his forehead, up through his hair

"Let's go, there's no point in hanging around all day." As they walked slowly back up the street they both were digesting their own private thoughts. Their failure was so obvious: like an F on a school paper. On reaching the main door of their house, they were both looking at the pavement. Alex turned to Francis and stared at him. For what seemed like ages, she said nothing. He was dumbfounded, when suddenly she said, "penguins."

"Penguins?" he asked, totally confused.

"Yes, penguins, Francis. Penguins!"

"Ok. I think you should go sit down, Alex."

"No, listen a moment. I love penguins, and that's what we should be thinking about to enter the shop. Don't you get it, I really love penguins," she said.

"Yes, Alex, but I don't love penguins."

"Doesn't matter. I love penguins and that's all that matters. We should both be thinking about them."

"Whatever you say," he agreed, shaking his head. They started towards the shop again.

"Penguins are beautiful creatures, simply the greatest things ever. God, I love them. The big ones, fat ones, not forgetting the little cute babies all covered in fluff," Alex shouted, laughing.

For a moment he was a little embarrassed by her outburst. In times of trouble, pulling strange faces always helped him.

Sticking his teeth out from his mouth as far as possible he announced to the world.

"You're right, they are absolutely beautiful." He sounded like an eighty-year-old women. His whole face strained under the stress. It was hilarious. More important they started to forget and didn't realise they had forgotten while simply enjoying the moment. Marching down the street towards the shop Alex was waving her hands like a conductor controlling some invisible orchestra.

"PENGUINS!" Francis screamed, seeing in his mind a vast open expanse of pure white snow. Marching forward were millions of tiny black and white dots. Penguins had done their hard time on this planet, rising up to take their place among the rulers of mother earth. Rocking from side-to-side destroying all in their path, penguins had taken over, literally. People on the street began transforming into penguins. The number 42 bus went buzzing past and Francis could have sworn the driver was a penguin. Alex was still shouting penguins as they rounded the corner and walked straight into the open shop. Before they knew it, they were standing in front of the counter.

"Well, it's about time you two. Thought you were never coming back," she exclaimed with joy as she came stomping out to greet them. Eloïse flung her arms around Alex and for a moment Francis didn't know what to do. After hugging Eloïse, he started to smile. Immediately she started yapping.

"My word! You two really tried so hard to visit me, and how busy you have been. Lighting the candle and seeing the other world." They both glanced at each other, feeling nervous. "Oh yes, you two, I know exactly what you've been getting up to."

"You do?" Francis moaned, shocked.

"Every last little detail. You couldn't hide that magic from a sorceress like me. Don't underestimate the power of that candle. Every bitch, sorry every witch in the city," she quickly corrected herself, "has been calling me since you lit it. My tag is on it," she said proudly. Francis and Alex stood motionless. Eloïse suddenly realised she may have frightened them a little and tried to change the subject.

The remark instantly sparked his paranoia, making him think about the stone in his pocket. Eloïse seemed to know even what was on his mind.

"Alex, pick a small gift for your parents from the shop. I want to have a chat with Francis." Alex looked at them both and understood it was meant to be a private conversation, but still ran off smiling. Eloïse then took a deep breath and sat back into the tall stool behind the counter, placing her arms on the rests. She looked at the pencil she'd picked up tapping it a few times on the wooden counter top. The silence was deadly. Francis was about to talk when she said, "Has the stone been talking to you?"

"What do you mean?" he questioned, now slightly on edge.

"Well, there are a few things I never got to tell you regarding the stone. More importantly, what's inside it?"

"Ah . . . well there were a couple of questions I wanted to ask you," he replied.

"If I was to ask you to give me the stone back and forget everything, would you?" she asked.

"Yeah no worries, you can have it back." He tossed it onto the counter in front of her. Eloïse looked straight through him feeling the pain he was already starting to enjoy.

"Francis, she is a child of the universe, free as the wind, warm as summer sun, and crazy as a March hare."

"Like me," he quickly snapped back at her.

"Yes, Francis but she . . ." Eloïse was surprised by his response.

"Is exactly like me," his response was firm and resounding.

Eloïse pushed the stone back across the counter top to him.

"So long as you know what you're doing Francis. You will find out she has been in that form for a long time, and for a very good reason," she cautioned.

Picking the stone up and saying nothing he smiled as Alex came running to the counter with a present she had picked out for their parents. Alex started to tell Eloïse all about the events of the last two days. With Alex doing most of the talking, Francis relaxed and only added some detail to the conversation when needed. Eloïse had assured them the other world was safe but after they told her what had happened in the bathroom, with the air all around them exploding, she suggested avoiding the beach area altogether as what normally happened there wasn't enjoyable anyway. She stressed that it was beautiful but also at times very uncomfortable if you don't really understand what's going on.

"The stones, especially the large ones, are renowned for having bad eyesight so be careful."

"Moving rocks," Francis shook his head in disbelief.

Alex started clenching her fists with excitement, as Eloïse continued.

"Well, it's like a holiday resort or unofficial home to lots of rocks and stones. Not all can walk and talk but they're all so interesting to look at and the stories, my God, they have seen such things. They know the history of the whole universe. The candle I gave you is a copy, but I made it myself. I went there to learn what happened in the past."

Suddenly questions were flying from both of them.

"What kind?

"How large?"

"Do they speak English?" and, of course, "What the hell do they do?"

"They sit on the beach all day and play their games. As will your stone, Francis. That's why I wanted to have a chat. She will play extremely dangerous games on the beach. It's simply what they do."

Eloïse came from behind the counter. Putting her arms around them both, she walked towards the door. Francis felt better and apologised for sounding so on edge.

"That's fine Francis; I was looking out for you."

"What game will she play, Eloïse?" he asked, concerned.

"You will find out. Maybe she will, maybe she won't. Who knows? Don't forget there are plenty of games people play that don't involve balls."

With that remark Francis' trust in Eloïse grew a little as he understood it to mean take it easy, which was already proving almost impossible.

"Oh, before I forget, promise me whatever happens don't look at, play with, suggest anything about, touch or talk . . . to the crabs."

"The crabs?" Francis looked surprised.

"They are without question the most untrustworthy bunch of criminals you'll ever meet on any world. Obtaining magical objects of any kind is all they're after. Even listening for longer than a moment will end in trouble."

"Crabs . . . *talking* crabs," Alex said.

"Yes, my dear and the pinch . . . from a larger solider crab. It's not worth the trouble. Seriously though, you two, the beach is teaming with magic. Under every stone is something completely different. During summer school, I spent a few weekends there for study. So if you are to have the same experience you will need these."

Opening her palm, two silver bracelets appeared from nowhere, instantly.

"Bring them every single time you visit the other world. They will normalise your appearance to all who see you." Her tone was serious. "Now off with you," she urged, pushing them out the door. They were so overjoyed with the magical gifts immediately they put them on running up the hill.

Later that evening, everything was proceeding according to their simple plan. Nothing had changed in the three days since they had received the candle from Eloïse. Francis stood at the edge of the bath, looking at the water where mountains of pure white foam started calling to him.

It's the most beautiful picture you could ever have wished for, he would whisper under his breath. *Maybe it was, maybe it wasn't. Who knows, and who cares? It's fantastic being here.*

Francis stood ready for the trip to this new world, alongside his sister who was dressed for winter. He had two t-shirts and a rain jacket on, in case. Turning off the water, he moved away from the bath as Alex entered the room. In her readiness to light the candle, she was so excited that she tossed her small shoulder bag onto the ground. What fell from the open bag caused Francis to laugh.

"Are you sure you have enough there Alex? I mean, could you not fit anything else in?"

Wholly involved in lighting the candle, Alex ignored the remark. Feeling tense and excited Francis watched. Having dreamed of this moment all day, never once had it left their mind, they looked to the ceiling waiting for it to start. Nothing on this earth could keep them from being there; both gazing towards the ceiling through the steam from the hot bath water.

"Do you see anything?" Alex asked. "No, be quiet. You know it takes time."

To Alex it always seemed ages before anything happened. And finally when it arrived they both stood there, still as stones. When it started, Francis was thinking of his father's classical music.

"With classical music, you are forced to think and can dream easier. You don't have to listen to words to feel emotion," he had told him on many occasions.

Now, after having looking at the bathroom ceiling for the last two days, he understood. Alex, on the other hand, didn't think of music. She was thinking like a lollypop that had been pulled from a freezer frozen solid.

"Can you see it moving?" he whispered.

"Where, I can't see anything?" Alex snapped.

"It's the beach. My God there are thousands of them, listen can you hear?"

"Are they singing?" Alex whispered.

Whatever was happening made no difference. Both of them were transfixed by the image on the ceiling. Maybe they are talking not singing he thought. You couldn't make sense of the shapes as the image was blurred most of the time. Some were large, others seemed tiny like a nest of marching ants on the warpath. Then abruptly the sound stopped.

"What was that?" she asked.

With no real idea of what it was, he couldn't answer. This time, something was different, very different. Without warning, the image on the ceiling completely collapsed around them. Worse still, they were simultaneously in the middle of the bathroom. Looking about, it seemed they were now standing in the middle of a street with their bathtub and part of the floor.

"Oh my God," she said terrified as she held the end of the bathtub tightly.

Slowly, as panic started to set in, Francis lowered his body down beside the protection of the heavy steel tub. A massive lump of what seemed like slate hobbled past like an old man. Alex staring at this fumbling giant slowly lowered her body also. At that point, in a desperate bid to hide his fears. Francis lowered his head pretending to look for some lost belonging. *What should I do?* he thought, terrified that the creature might bite off his head.

Finally when it had passed, Francis raised his head and was shocked to see Alex splashing another human node creature of stone walking past.

"Stop Alex, what are you doing? You will get us into trouble!" he shouted.

"Don't worry, they can't see us. Look!" she grinned.

Tossing another handful of water at what looked like a half a ton of limestone. You would never have seen the like. The creatures were made of stone but had the basic shape of humans with arms, legs and faces with expressions.

With no reaction from the creatures they had a sudden change of fortune. Moments later, both of them were tossing water at everything passing by. They could not stop laughing, it was so much fun. Yet as suddenly as it started, it stopped. The connection with this strange world was abruptly broken by what sounded like a headless chicken running down Grafton Street on a Saturday morning covering everyone with blood.

"FRANCISSS!" their mother screamed from the bottom of the stairs.

Instantly they were reminded of home. Alex quickly blew out the candle. Incredibly the veil that covered the walls of the bathroom reversed its journey backwards taking the weird creatures with it leaving only the plain white solid walls of their bathroom.

Together, they turned around to see the total shock on their mum's face. Nobody was laughing now, realising that the water tossed at the creatures was not on the street of the strange new world, but all over the bathroom floor. She was absolutely furious with them. Though secretly she hoped for neither, after all that had happened in the bathroom over the last two days, his mother must have imagined that Francis was now making bombs or smoking drugs. He started making up excuses about the taps being left on as he exited the room repeating "sorry" at least ten times. His mother reminded him that he was going to clean up the mess now without any delay. He returned with another two towels and started to mop up. As soon as their mum was downstairs Alex entered Francis's room looking relieved.

"Get the candle, we have to do it right now," he insisted.

"What! Mum will have our heads."

"I don't care. I'm going now." He couldn't possibly realise how that sounded to Alex. Nothing was going to keep him from going tonight.

"I'm not waiting a fucking week to go," he stated calmly, while tying his shoe laces.

He was thinking like someone who was trapped in a bottle that at any moment would explode. He knew it would be difficult to escape because he himself had tightened the bottle top and trapped all those lustful emotions inside. Like when you open a flacon of Chanel No. 5 from Ernest Beaux you can receive the sensation of rolling around in some lush green meadow with your lover, or a mind freezing uncontrolled explosion that's directly linked to something that happened in a person's past.

Alex had the same habit of raising her hand to rub her eyes and forehead as Francis when she was growing impatient.

"God! Quickly stuff some clothes under your bed sheets, make it look like you're asleep," he said

She then returned to her own room and did the same. With the lights off their Mum was sure to think they were fast asleep, especially after the explosion last night. Grabbing some extra clothes and such, Francis left the door ajar. Excited and gripped with fear, forced both of them to forget about any trouble regarding their parents.

"But if we get caught, Mum will kill us," Alex said

"Doesn't matter. We go now."

By the expression on her face he knew she understood his urge to leave and perhaps all the things he hadn't told her about the stone and what he really wanted. Francis turned the shower on so the room was fast filling with steam from the hot water. After a few moments it was wall-to-wall steam, but looked great, Alex remarked laughing. With the shower now off he asked her to hold the candle.

"All clear," she whispered, crossing the room.

"Hold still, while I light it," he asked. Alex was looking round the room, saying, "I can't see anything at all, there's so much steam."

"Be quiet, or Mum will hear us," he snapped.

It took only a few moments and the room took on a magical glow. Every star in the heavens were right at this very moment in their bathroom, at number 46 North Great George's Street.

"It could be night time. It's so dark."

Alex looked very worried at the prospect. Frankly Francis was more frightened of his mother walking thought the door than anything else.

"I'm scared Francis," Alex admitted.

"Don't worry we will be fine. Sure we even have the magical wrist bands from Eloïse," he told her, reassuringly.

They both peered at the beautiful orange flame flickering back and forth. The steam had now totally engulfed the room, as he grabbed her hand firmly. They knew they were about to leave a warm bathroom, but they were also aware they were somewhere else and it was cold, very cold, as Francis blew out the candle.

"Oh Alex, what have I done?" he sounded worried as hell. With that, they both vanished from the room.

Chapter Six

THE NEW WORLD

Alex stood shivering in the darkness. Francis didn't look any better.

"Mum is going to execute us," she said.

"Why did I do that? I don't understand. Why the hell did I light that damn candle?" he kept repeating aloud. It took a few yanks on his arm from Alex to stop him blabbering.

"Francis, how the hell are we going to get back?" she nervously asked.

It took a few moments for both of them to relax and get some bearings. They repeated what Eloïse had said, that by relighting the candle and thinking of home, they could easily return. Everything was so strange. All the buildings had a differently shaped door, not like at home in Dublin. It seemed that the doors were in the shape of the creature that lived inside: some were thin; others fat and again some looked like a creature had walked straight through the wall. Although both of them were a little frightened, this crazy wondrous sight had brought an unexpected smile to their faces and helped them relax.

"Let's walk a little, Alex, look around some. Eloïse said this place is perfectly safe."

Alex was still holding firm to his arm as they walked towards the end of the street. With no noise they felt very uneasy. It was like walking in the countryside, with the light of the full moon covering everything in a soft dim light. Each house had only one window, not very nice for the owners, he thought.

"Listen, Francis. What's that noise?"

Turning his head to the side he attempted to understand it, give it a name; anything to relate to something he recognised but nothing came to mind.

"It's coming from up the street, think we should take a look," he enquired.

Both of them crept up along the left side of a wall that ran half the length of the street. Alex kept glancing up over to Francis biting her lower lip. Slowly they came to a stop realising about ten meters away was an enormous giant creature that resembled granite; this wasn't exactly what you'd call *normal*. It was rocking back and forth a few inches while making the strangest noise.

"What's it doing?" Alex asked.

"Don't know, but looks stuck."

The creature was the size of a car and had the basic form of a man: two thick legs, arms and a large head gave it the appearance of a giant. Its left foot was half in a puddle of water, which the creature seemed unable to escape from.

"I think it might need some help," she said.

"You might be right. But the thing is HUGE. How do we know it won't hurt us?"

"Eloïse never said they were dangerous to talk to, not like the crabs, only that they had terrible eyesight," Alex reminded him.

"Ok, but let me do the talking, all right?" he responded sternly.

Slowly they crept towards this monster. It was crouched over, staring down at its foot in the water. Circling around so as to approach it head on, they stopped talking. Apart from the soft moaning from the creature the night was calm and still.

"Eh, excuse me, sir, but can we help?" Francis said politely looking at the creature.

For a moment he assumed it hadn't heard, so was about to ask again when its head started moving. The noise was like two giant boulders grinding against each other. Its head, at least three feet across, came slowly up to his level as it was crouching on its left knee. Scared out of their wits, Francis and Alex stood motionless. Alex's hand was attached to her brother like a vise grip.

Even though the creature was made of stone you could easily make out the pale blue colour of its eyes. Its mouth was open but nothing was coming out. This went on for a few moments. At this stage, even Alex wanted to talk but couldn't find the words. For some reason Francis was thinking of trees blowing in the wind; probably because it's a nice image, no stress! As the creature moved its head again, his daydreaming was abruptly halted.

Francis seemed to know the creature was aware of the stone in his pocket. The creature's eyes winced and suddenly Francis's leg started burning. Quickly reaching into his pocket, he removed the stone. In his open palm it was now warm. The creature pulled back his head startled, or so it seemed.

"*Youuuu,*" it said with a very deep tone.

"Sorry, I don't understand. Do you speak English?" Francis asked.

It looked directly at him as he returned the stone to his pocket. Alex was about to say something from her two years of French class when a noise came from underneath the creature's foot.

"Hey I do. Perfect English but so does my friend. He's a bit surprised at meeting you," said the voice.

The granite monster pushed down with its heavy foot and the voice was submerged under the water. You could see little bubbles popping out; releasing coloured light that sparkled for a moment then disappeared.

"They don't seem to be friendly. Let's get the hell out of here." Francis said, already turning to walk away dragging his sister.

But the creature's foot started moving out of the water again. This time being pushed.

"No don't leave, we're the best of friends," said the voice.

By degrees, they realised it was a crab under this massive walking piece of granite.

"It's a crab! Jesus, Alex it's a crab. How could the crab possibly be so strong?"

"It's . . . incredible," she started muttering.

To their amazement, the crab was managing to remove the creature's foot completely out of the water, and the ten ton walking monster appeared unable to stop him. Both Alex and Francis had moved a few steps back now. As the massive granite creature came crashing down to earth, they were equally frightened and astonished by what they were witnessing.

Right after which the crab leapt from the water and started talking to Francis as if nothing had happened. In fact, he winked at Alex in a manner which alarmed Francis. Dumbfounded by the fact that a little four inch tall crab was making conversation could not describe the internal workings of their young brains. With the granite monster now standing, it was a simply too much excitement. The crab starting pulling at Francis' trousers with one of his claws demanding to see what he had in his pocket.

"It's only something belonging to me," Francis assured him.

The crab started laughing while turning to look at the monstrous piece of granite behind him.

"I don't want to sound unfriendly, but you're crazy, if you think I believe that."

For a moment everyone felt uncomfortable, like some awkward meeting of strangers in a quiet pub.

"Ok, I should start again. I apologise for being so forward. What's your name anyway?" asked the crab, cheerily.

"What's yours?" Francis replied with a smirk.

Stunned, he saw the expression on the crab's face. It actually looked like he was offended by the remark. It pointed with its extra large claw towards the piece of granite behind him.

"Ok. Let's start over a second time. My name is Herman and this big lump is Smasher, my dear friend."

"Ok. My name is Francis and this is my younger sister Alex."

Everyone started to calm down. Francis and Alex now understood the crab and his friend were messing about with each other.

"How did you manage to push your friend away? You're so small," Alex asked.

"Well my dear, firstly you can call me Herman and, in answer to your question, magic. But you must know something of this world because your brother is carrying a really hot piece of magic in his pocket. Something that is bound to get him a HUGE amount of attention, if he doesn't release her soon."

Francis' mind was questioning how this crab knew so much about the stone.

"Look, you seem to be new around here so how about a cup of tea back at Smasher's house? It's around the corner," Herman suggested.

Alex was up for it as she was freezing, but Francis was slightly more cautious. Reluctantly he agreed but let them lead. Watching Herman walk, Francis started to smile, the little crab moved sideways making a funny clatter. Only then did they both notice that his skinny stick-like legs had silver rings that knocked against each other. Alex started to laugh and relaxed a little now that the conversation had turned to more normal topics.

"Excuse me, Herman but how big is Smasher's house? I'm curious because he's SO big."

"Well, if you two hang around long enough I will fill you in as best I can, ok?" he stated firmly.

It was still a little unnerving talking to Herman for both of them. His mouth moved from side to side as he spoke, not up and down like normal people, but it was hard to tell considering he was five feet shorter. He wasn't a person; he was a crab, and a *talking* crab at that. In fact, he hadn't stopped talking since they met him.

"When did you arrive? How long are you staying? Where are you from? Any friends with you . . . ?" He went on.

It was impossible to answer so many questions. Alex simply gave up trying. Thankfully, when they reached Smasher's house everything slowed down. Smasher, the ten foot tall lump of granite, was the first to reach the door of a very large bungalow.

Herman snapped his right claw a few times. The noise was quite loud.

"As you two are new, I will elaborate. Smasher is a moving rock and he likes living in a house of sorts. His house has an entrance like normal buildings. No door as such, though, only a covering of a blanket because stones don't like those doors."

Smasher went in followed quickly by Herman who waved his claw at Francis and Alex attempting to convince them it was safe. With the covering pulled back, the entrance opened to a lovely large sitting room, where everything was made of stone. Further back you could see another two coverings along part of the wall which must have lead to other rooms.

Smasher offered them tea and bid them to sit down. Nothing had prepared them for this: a stone drinking tea. Everyone made themselves comfortable while Smasher walked into the darkness towards the back of this very large, one roomed house. Alex was asking Herman questions about everything you could imagine. "How does the magic work? How can a crab speak English?"

After a while, when both Francis and Alex became overwhelmed by the events of the last hour, the conversation became unimportant.

Smasher returned with the tea and his huge head was again distracted by the contents of Francis' pocket. Francis pulled out the stone and placed it on the table. Herman stared at it. Smasher sat down in a chair the size of a normal kitchen table.

"Where did you find it? Were you given it? Or did you know nothing of it and this is where you are now?" Herman asked.

"Yes! Yes!" Alex shouted, elated.

"We met a witch in our world and she suggested we come here," Francis continued.

Alex pulled at his sleeve and gave him a disappointed stare.

"Well, she's not really a witch. More like a female wizard of sorts," Herman laughed while tossing his claw victoriously into the air.

"Francis, you do know what you are carrying in your pocket? As you both seem like really friendly humans, I can only imagine that this female wizard, whoever she is, told you about it. I mean that whatever lies within the stone is part of you. It's your making, like a mirror image."

"Well . . . mostly," Francis said with a sigh.

"Then I must ask you, Francis, has she been talking to you?" Herman added in a soft, childish voice shaking his head.

Embarrassed and lost for words Francis had to admit that it felt like they were together a few months. He took no offence at the crab's remark. Alex knew nothing of what had been happening regarding the stone and the even stranger connection Francis had with it.

"Well, yes, she has," he replied softly, looking at the ground.

"Jesus, you're going out with a stone, that's brilliant," Alex said laughing.

"Listen up Francis, that's totally normal for this type of stone, and . . . as you seem none the worse, you should free her immediately. If you feel safe with her then you should to do it now."

Moments later Francis was standing in one of the back rooms with the stone in almost total darkness, his heart pumping fast. It was too late for second thoughts. He now wanted to touch the dream of the last few days, if that's what was supposed to happen. Dropping the stone into a container of water it instantly started expanding. The stone began emitting beautiful golden strikes of light that flashed across his eyes as he fell to his knees. The shape of a face inside the stone appeared again like it had in Eloïse's shop. The bubble of water grew larger and larger which made him nervous.

Her eyes, piercing black, were upon him as she slowly started to transform into a real girl, emerging like a diver from some deep, still ocean; breaking through the thin bubble of water which resembled cling film. He was drenched by the water as she fell into his open arms. Her scent was now covering his entire body, utterly overpowering. Like being wrapped in a blanket of pleasure. They hugged each other tightly. They knew each other. Francis was aware she held a part of him and he could feel it. Jesus Christ had reunited two angles after a lifetime of separation. Distance was a plane in space, and space had been folded over on itself. She had no clothes on: Starkers!

Water was flowing from her hair over her shoulders and down her back. She had the strangest skin Francis had ever touched: firm like marble, yet soft as only a lover knows. Slowly he released his grip and pushed her back. She appeared weak and only half-opened her eyes. Relaxed, she rested her head on his shoulder in a tight embrace of affection.

Doors generally have locks for reasons; Francis knew this girl was a key of sorts. Exactly what it could be used to open he had no idea. Steam was rising from her body, twisting slowly around her, as the water evaporated off her now warmer skin. From one beautiful moment to another she was stunning. He craved the dry heat from her body. It was like being next to a miniature nuclear generator. He imagined being a little electron spinning around this atom trapped in an embrace with no end. With every circumference of the atom he would touch this perfect creature. Licking it clean until nothing else mattered. Delight was a forgotten word from a civilization in some far off corner of empty space.

Francis kissed her on the cheek like a real gentleman. He realised he had to find something to cover her. Looking around the room, he helped her to her feet and led her to what looked like a floor bed with some folded blankets.

Chapter Seven

THE SAME PERSON

Smasher made his way into the room after knocking on the wall beside its entrance. Followed by Alex and Herman who was scurrying across the floor. They seemed concerned. Alex came straight to Francis reaching out with her hand. His smile seemed reassuring and that was enough for her, even though he was hiding so many of his feelings.

"Is she alright?" Herman asked.

"I think so, yeah."

At this point, Francis was well over the edge of the cliff regarding his emotional attachment to her. His mind transformed his stress to take the shape of a bright red sports car approaching the cliff at a hundred miles an hour. That beauty wasn't going over in slow motion, doors wide open trying to fly screaming at its impending faith. He had already fast-forwarded himself to striking the base of the cliff, laying there as each new wave pounded over his body bringing relief, like a slap in the face to keep him awake. He had no other option but to go with the flow given that no other alternative was clear. He so wanted to collapse into bed with her for a week, but that simply wouldn't be enough. Herman and Smasher seemed to be taking a great deal of interest in her. Smasher was repeatedly speaking to Herman in a language unknown to humans.

"Do you know her, Herman?" Francis asked.

"Yes! Believe it or not, I do. I can't begin to guess how long it's been."

"Tell me about her. I don't even know her real name. I've been calling her Gem. Well that's what I felt like calling her." he explained.

"Well, Francis, you already know a lot as she is part you."

Smasher looked over her she wasn't injured. Herman asked the rest of them to return to the living room so as to continue the conversation. He spoke like they were friends and at one point it was obvious she was someone that was respected.

"Francis many creatures have found Gem, as you call her, over the years. She's had many names also, but a new beginning demands something different, so Gem it is. Others have discarded her as they had no understanding of what she was. Some of the creatures that understood her made promises that never came to be. You released her without any conditions because you wanted her to be free. It's happened with her that she has been used and torn apart by many things, such as greed and lust alike. You're the first and this can only be a good thing."

Alex was quiet for the first time since Francis could remember. She was too busy listening. The slight rattle of Herman's rings when he moved a leg caused her to smile with excitement. Eventually, Herman stopped moving altogether in any direction. Alex was dying to speak but understood she needed to let him finish. Smasher returned from the other room and assured everyone, in English, that Gem was well and asleep. He then proceeded to toss wood into the fireplace. After which, Herman extended a claw from which sparks flew. Suddenly, the fire was blazing.

Both Francis and Alex spent the next hour listening to Herman with intense interest. The conversation was about everything regarding this world: magic rings, stones, the games, human visitors. Herman explained that they didn't get many humans this time of year and, when they did, mostly they stayed at the far end of the beach about a mile away. Smasher raised his hand to his open mouth in the gesture of eating and both Francis and Alex understood. Raising his huge body he walked off into the darkness down a passageway to the left of where Gem was sleeping. Moments later, you could hear the clatter of objects falling about. Some sounded like they must have weighed half a ton. Everyone looked at each other questioningly but they could see nothing until he emerged again carrying a sack full of rice. Alex laughed. Smasher was totally unaware at how much humans eat. Alex then proceeded to cook two small handfuls in a little pot on the fire.

All this time Francis could hear whispers in his head, which most certainly were coming from Gem in the other room. Alone and silent, she was still talking to him. It was nothing like the connection of the last few days. Now they seemed like echoes of confused conversations that nobody remembers. Smasher turned his head towards the door and Alex stood up as if expecting someone to enter. She looked to Francis.

"It's a crab."

"Well, you are both full of surprises. Alex, you will have to explain how you knew that sometime?" Herman remarked, as he turned to face Smasher.

"Hello!" stated the crab while entering the room very discreetly. He walked directly over to Herman.

They didn't talk, but communicated by moving their claws up and down. Some moments later he left as quietly as he had entered and Herman returned his attention to Francis and Alex.

"Francis, please tell me more about how you came to be here?"

"We found Gem. Met up with Eloïse and she said go have some fun."

At this point, Alex removed the candle from her bag and showed it to everyone. Smasher began swinging his head from side to side in what appeared to be disbelief. Dust began falling to the ground from his neck area.

"You two really have come prepared. May I see that for a moment?" he said

Alex opened her mouth about a second before Francis and started chatting. In fact she forgot herself and told the whole story of the last week. Gratefully giving less detail regarding the connection her brother had with Gem, details of which Francis still found a little too embarrassing to discuss in front of everyone. Smasher had ground together two large rocks to salt their rice, heavily.

Once they'd eaten the rice, Herman suggested that they return home for the night or sleep a few hours here. Tomorrow they would get The Grand Tour.

Alex was jumping with excitement at this. Francis was still listening to the calls from the other room. Not to mention the fact they had both disappeared from their bathroom in the middle of the night. God only knows what their mother and father were going through right now. For all they knew, both of their children could be dead. Herman talked to Alex as she lay on the floor in a makeshift bed for at least an hour, yapping until she fell asleep. Francis left for Gem's room, happy all was well with his sister. He thanked Herman for treating himself and his sister Alex so kindly and retired. Upon pulling the cover over the entrance to the room he realised he wouldn't be leaving for hours.

Walking slowly over to where she was laying he knew they had been friends for years, even longer. He opened the long fingers of his right hand and placed them right above her belly button. She felt warm but still that slight feeling of marble. It was abnormally surreal as they lay facing each other. Slowly they came closer until their foreheads touched, and that's where they stayed for a least an hour. They didn't say a word; like comatose patients in a hospital they were busy in silence. Placing both his hands around her cheeks and holding her head tight he kissed her like the sea kisses a tropical island on a sunny day. The wind was warm and the trees lush green. His eyes were focused on her youthful lips. The dry imperfections to which he wished to add moisture. Himself as the ocean, he imagined gentle waves flowing onto and over her lips. Like all waves gravity pulls them back as the water rushed passed her white imperfectly shaped teeth returning once again to that great bounty of life that is the sea. Francis thought he felt somehow older around her. This was how he fell asleep that night dreaming beside someone who sounded like they were not breathing.

When he awoke the next morning, his eyes were clear and bright. Moving slowly as he had no idea what to expect. But everything was fine. In fact he sat right up to fall back down into what he assumed was his bed. Gem stirred, turned round to him with her half-open eyes, lent forward and laid a kiss gently on his lips.

"Thank you for respecting me," she said.

"No worries, I'm happy you asked me under the covers."

The moment of understanding had arrived for both of them. Trust.

"So what are we going to do today?" she asked.

"How about a relaxing day on the beach?" he suggested, smiling.

"Sounds great," she answered.

Francis was about to pull the covers over both of them when, to his shock, he realised there weren't any covers and he actually wasn't in his bed.

"Oh my God. Oh my God! Alex, Alex!" he screamed.

"What's up with you, Francis?"

He jumped to his feet pulling his t-shirt over his head.

"I will be back in a few hours, need to check everything is ok in my world."

Stumbling around the room, searching for his runners, he tossed the extra pair of jeans and a shirt he brought beside Gem. Kissing her, he left shouting for his sister.

Alex was already up with everything ready. She had no time for questions as to why her brother was sleeping with a stone. Francis was a mess. Shoelaces untied, trousers hanging off his waist.

"Light it!" He demanded.

"Slow down, it's not me that's late. Do you think they're up?"

"No idea, what time is it?"

"Seven, maybe," Alex replied.

As this strange world slowly transformed into their bathroom, both of them dreaded the thought of explaining everything to their mother. Materialising as they did beside the bath tub, they both held their breath waiting for the police to come charging into the room.

Timidly, they walked towards the half open door. Gestures became the new form of communication. Pulling back the door Francis silently peeked about. Nodding ok to his sister, they both crept for their bedrooms and peace. Entering his room, he ripped the covers from his bed, and quietly tossing to the floor the clothes that had been his body double like a fisherman discards the head of a fish. Collapsing into its familiar warmth, he rolled in its glory and Gem's smell. Within minutes, both Francis and his sister fell into a deep sleep.

It was around 10:00 a.m. when Francis woke to his mother pulling at his bed covers. She couldn't see the pile of clothes on the opposite side of the bed that had been thrown to the floor only a few hours ago. He shouted at her to leave him alone which was their normal routine. After breakfast was over, Alex suggested they say they would be going to a friend's house for the day. Their mother should think nothing of that. Since their father was at work they waited until she left for the shops first. Both of them scrambled about the kitchen taking bread, cheese and water in their packs.

Alex started laughing at the fact that she had forty-seven unread text messages on her mobile phone. She hadn't used it for the last few days and was sure her friends were venting their frustration as to why she was missing from their lives. Tomorrow she'd spend the day reading them. Having fooled their parents so well last night, they were already going back right now, although they had only returned a few hours ago. Five minutes later they had transported back onto the street near Smasher's house.

"Shit! I forgot the sun block," Francis said aloud.

"Then we say we were at the beach all day," Alex explained.

Walking down the street, they could have been mistaken for tourists, wandering around aimlessly, enjoying the city and its people. When they arrived at the front of Smasher's house they noticed the little window to the left, more like a stone missing from the wall, and what seemed like a flower box, but no flowers, only this beautiful light green ivy growing up along the side of the window towards the roof.

Gem came out to meet them both. Francis kissed Gem and was finding it hard to hide his happiness. They all chatted about the last few days. Alex asked Gem was she all right, informing her that the incident at Eloïse's shop was a little crazy.

"I'm sorry you both had to see that. That's what happens sometimes," Gem added.

"Did you really call to me that day on the beach?" Alex asked.

"Yes, I did. Francis was unable to hear me so I tried you. Eloïse wanted us to meet, I mean Francis and myself."

"Why did she want you to meet me of all people?"

"Because she knew we could help each other Francis," Gem replied. Alex looked confused, indicating that she wanted to know more.

"I've been missing a long time so not too sure what's going on."

"No worries, we can sort all that out later. Shall we check out the beach?" Francis beamed from one side of his mouth to the other.

Alex was so excited she started walking. Secretly, Francis couldn't wait but was holding back his emotions again. He smiled broadly. It seemed to make no difference to him. All his concentration was focused on Gem as they chatted together walking along. Alex kept her distance a little ahead. It sounded like complete rubbish but somehow every word they said made perfect sense. Gem knew as much about this world as she did about Dublin, Europe and mankind.

She spoke good English like any normal European except Francis couldn't quite make out if it was French or Belgium because of the slight accent. When she spoke it was playful with undertones of someone who was very alert. He didn't even have time to ask her where she had lived except that she must have lived at sometime in Europe. Didn't matter anyway as they were totally engrossed in their conversation, laughing at each other's comments regarding a building they were passing.

"No, no, the building is used for the transportation of Germans who have been accused of being too German by the Germans themselves and that's where they end up," he said, throwing a wide-eyed sarcastic glance in her direction.

"Or the house is for any Spanish living in Dublin. Some secret US organisation kidnaps them, messes with their heads to make them more Spanish to see how long it takes them to go crazy. It's meant to be used as a drug in some future wars off in Africa," she suggested.

"Wait, wait I got it. It's the first alien incursion on earth. Holy shit! They have this huge bunker under the building with laboratories and such. Anybody who enters is scanned by a futuristic device at the door to see if they have the right profile for what they need. So far they discovered that the French were best suited to pissing off the Irish," he suggested.

"The French?" she questioned.

"Yeah, the aliens want to take Ireland first as it's an easy target and use the French as a wedge to tip the Irish people into a revolution and, in the following chaos, take control. See the Irish are too lazy to do anything at all and the French will show them all their flaws so they make those French. . . French extreme."

"You're really nuts." Gem was holding her stomach tight as her laughing was out of control.

"What if . . . all those different plans were happening and none of them knew each other were operating from the same building because they were so secretive?

Experiments sometimes go wrong, and the mishaps get thrown into a cellar from all the groups, and they end up forming another secret organisation leading to . . ." she paused.

At this moment, Francis's tongue almost lolled from the side of his mouth, excreting drool. Thankfully, he had enough self-control and kept this little daydream to himself. His eyes were wide open and wet because this woman was perhaps crazier than himself and he definitely found that attractive.

Herman appeared waiting in the middle of the path. He greeted Alex who was a little ahead. They had left the so-called town about two hundred metres behind them and started to climb a small sand dune leading to the beach. Francis couldn't wait any longer, so popped the question.

"Gem, where are you really from?"

"Well, that's a bit of a long story . . . I will tell you. But not right now," she said with such a lovely smile. "There's something over this hill I haven't seen in a very long time and I really want you to enjoy it as much as me. You know what's coming Francis, and I will share it with you."

"Yeah, you gotta tell me about those images I'm being consumed with the last few days," he admitted.

"Well it wasn't only me that was messing around the last few days. I saw so much from inside you that I had to stop."

Gem started laughing. She noticed Francis looked a little worried but she soon put him at ease.

"It's what you have inside your head that frightened me. Well, to be completely honest, Francis I like the way you think. It's an insanely intense feeling being surrounded by your thoughts."

"Yeah, I have a similar problem with that," he continued while secretly his thoughts caused him to blush slightly.

"I adore my dreams the last few days. Together with you in bed . . . it's amazing and exhausting."

Chapter Eight

THE BEACH

Nothing in Francis's life so far had prepared him for the sight he was about to witness with Alex. It was beyond his imagination – Eloïse had said. Expect that she had forgotten to mention it was really beyond reason. Almost everything was moving as far as the eye could see. Stones of every conceivable shape were rambling around like any human would on a normal beach. Alex was, well, speechless. Francis thought she was overcome by the sight. Shocked, she turned to Francis and then back to the beach. For a moment, like Francis, she was full of emotion. Francis talked to her but was still looking at the beach and all that his mind could accept.

"We now know life is everywhere."

It seemed like some strange landscape shown on a NASA web page depicting what the surface of Mars resembles on a bad day. Except this sky was so perfectly blue that you knew you were walking through a desert that runs to the sea. The horizon was melting from the heat, causing a shimmering effect on the creatures as they moved over the landscape in the distance. After they walked down along the other side of the embankment, it was flat sand for one hundred metres until what looked like a wall of stone. Alex was distracted by Herman hurrying along for some reason. In fact he started running, if that's what crabs do. Alex turned to the others surprised.

"It's ok. Let him go. It's how this area makes him feel that's getting to him," Gem continued. "This part of the beach is called The Dead Zone. The tears of millions of stones lost in time. Not the most appealing image for sure, and it definitely bugs Herman. In the water the sand can't communicate to him the way it is now." She put on a sorrowful smile. "The most powerful ring he has which keeps him alive so long, also reminds him of all those fallen in the past. Some are his friends, some enemies."

"Do you not feel anything, Gem?" Francis asked.

"Francis look!" Suddenly Alex interrupted, jumping nearer to his side. The sand was moving at their feet. It resembled a small molehill from a farmer's field, but moved like a wave ahead of them.

"Don't worry; it's only a gathering of sadness. Like a bunch of bad feelings coming together in someone's mind, nothing else. Continue walking and it will pass you by," Gem insisted.

"Wish I had my bloody video camera. My mates would kill to see this!" Francis said with visible disappointment.

Taking only a few minutes to cross this stretch of flat sand, they jumped onto solid ground. Herman was waiting for them and as Alex started to speak he abruptly stopped her.

"Please listen to me for a moment, Alex and Francis. You already know this is no normal beach as you can see and there is absolutely nothing normal about the creatures that live here. They can talk, walk and most important they are individuals. Nearly all have spent time in your world and have a great understanding about the universe, but they don't get the chance to chat to humans often, so go easy with them and you will, I am sure, earn their respect."

Francis glanced at Alex. They both took a moment and then nodded their heads in agreement. Herman begged them both to come closer and hold out their arms with the bracelets from Eloïse's shop. As he touched Alex's bracelet with his claw sparks started flying from it. He appeared to have gotten a small electric shock. Quickly releasing it, he apprehensively made his way to Francis' bracelet and was considerably more cautious. Unfortunately he was zapped again by what looked like a tiny flash of lightning. Nothing really hurtful but he was very surprised to have been zapped suddenly like that.

"Ok! That's the way it is then. Every single creature will know you are with me," he said shaking his head from the shock.

"What was all that about Herman?"

"It's an extra protection for you and your brother, Alex, like saying to everyone you are a guest of mine," he happily announced.

Alex thought how friendly this was of Herman though was unable to hug him the way she would normally hug a person, which put her in a bit of a position while giving Gem and Francis something to laugh about and Herman a feeling of acceptance; Alex gently stuck out her little finger. Herman took it with his claw and shook it in a gesture of friendship.

"Go discover the beach. I have business to attend and can't hang about." Herman pointed towards the beach.

Francis wondered what in God's name sort of business could a crazy talking crab with magical rings possibly be rushing off for? They all said goodbye to Herman and happily ventured out into wonderland.

On first seeing the beach from a distance, it had the appearance of watching a city from space, viewed from a satellite. It was absolutely teaming with life and you could feel the energy. Looking at Gem, Francis understood what she was feeling, like some place you visit when you're young, returning years later and remembering some meaningful forgotten emotion. She was so excited, carrying such a pretty smile he wanted to jump all over her. Placing his hand under her t-shirt, he rubbed her lower back. She quickly grabbed his hand and started swinging it through the air, as Francis pulled them together kissing her neck. This really made her smile. *Jesus this is so cool* he thought to himself. Alex was running to the first creature she liked the look of which happened to be a piece of basalt relaxing on a pile of lifeless stones.

"Hello!" Alex said eagerly.

"Hello to you," it answered.

"I'm new here and wanted to chat," she said.

"That's fine, I'm not new and would prefer to relax so please chat away; elsewhere."

The expression on Alex's face quickly changed to disappointment at the creature's rude response to her politeness. She stepped backwards towards the others.

"You'll meet all sorts in life in your world, so look at it in the same way Alex, the guy doesn't want to chat, so leave him alone," Gem suggested.

"Ok. I can do that," she firmly stated.

Everyone laughed. They continued down this narrow pathway, the hustle and bustle of the beach surrounded them completely. It was like some mad scientist had used a contraption to shrink them to the size of ants. Everything seemed massive and stronger. There were thousands of tiny stones beneath them hurrying around like some herd of wildebeests stretched across an African plain. More confusing for Francis was that the larger rocks came to that conclusion years ago and he knew it.

Sedimentary, metamorphic rocks of every kind, form and colour were going about their business. Francis walked above and beneath the shadows of giants. Gem squeezed tight on his hand. Looking to her he was sure that something was right about this.

"I don't like doing this, but you're a nice guy. You know that, don't you?"

"You mean holding hands," he questioned.

"Well yes, in public, it's not something I do a lot, but you make it easy, Francis."

Not for one moment did he stop to think. Why should he? He didn't have to and she felt exactly the same regarding how their relationship was speeding along. Why meddle with something that's working fine. Now that was a nice feeling he hadn't experienced too often; it kind of felt like being a young stream happy as hell to be born somewhere far off on a mountaintop, slowly meandering along, picking up this and that as it twists and turns towards its faith. Francis was, of course, dreaming about that stream when some beautiful sailing boat had been launched into his arms. He wouldn't be pushing against it.

Moreover it would be a pleasure to carry such a beautiful and vibrant craft towards the sea. At this stage he was nearly speaking to himself lost in a daydream. Once it reached the sea and started its maiden voyage across the great Atlantic, he would rest beneath its rib and lick its hull with every splash of water. When it slowed at the doldrums he would nestle up to its bosom, while softly caressing its perfect hull.

Upon arriving in the south Atlantic the boat would truly be rocking on top of him. Shaking his head, he started to laugh at these ridiculous thoughts.

"What's so funny?" Gem asked.

"Nothing, this place, it's nuts!!! Absolutely nuts."

"You like it. Good I knew you would. Thanks Francis, 'cause I have so many friends down on the beach I must introduce you to."

"For sure, Gem it would be a pleasure."

"Wait until you meet Neva. He's my best friend. If he doesn't like you, that's it." They both started laughing understanding the sarcasm.

After a while, they came to an incline and could finally see the ocean in its full glory. From this point it was mostly sand and scattered rocks up to the water's edge.

"That's strange, there are no stones in the water?" he found this surprising.

"I will explain all of this later. Really, there is so much to say I don't know how to start," Gem explained.

Alex had already taken off her shoes and was knee-deep in the crystal clear sea. Gem and Francis were still holding hands when she stopped dead a few feet from where small waves hit the beach. Abruptly, she pulled him back.

"I will give the skinny-dipping a miss for the moment, Francis, but please go for a swim if you like," she whispered.

"Come on, let's have some fun," he pulled her towards the water.

"No. I don't want to."

"What's up? Come on . . ." he continued pulling her.

"NO Francis. Don't force me. Really, DON'T!" she screamed releasing her hand. Clearly, she was extremely angry.

"Well ok. Sorry." Now he was slightly worried. Knowing well he had pissed her off, understandably he felt a little guilty. With any relationship in the beginning, you arrive at a point where a fight starts and true feelings come to the surface. She could have been a fish happily swimming under the water all her wonderful merry life then suddenly finding herself tossed on the rocks by an unnatural wave. This was a sign he should have recognised. The letters stretched twenty feet above his head on a massive neon red billboard stating: *It's too good, Francis. You're going to get hurt.* Unfortunately in life, it isn't always so easy to see what's directly before you, even when it's only two feet away.

Quietly, Gem said they should follow her up the beach after the swim. Her soft manner relaxed Francis the same way his sister's did. Maybe that's why he always had time for Alex. He knew that to date, most of the trouble in his life was a direct result of his own actions and no-one else: arguing with his parents over silly things like staying out late, getting into a fight at school, wanting more space. It was all part of the normal attitude of a young man growing up. That's the way the world worked.

Chapter Nine

THE COCK TAVERN

After the brief swim, Francis and Alex walked up the beach searching for Gem. Seeing the beach stretching off into the distance from the water's edge was such a beautiful sight. With the sun directly overhead, they realised there was almost no time difference between the beach and Dublin. It was like some scene from Rio, or Bondi beach in Australia, of which Francis had only seen images on TV, except here only the crabs were swimming in the water; some looked like they were playing games, others were relaxing in the sun like a bunch of humans on their holidays in Spain.

Gem greeted them with a smile followed by a soft touch to Francis's shoulder. Instantly he knew that all was as it should be and nothing needed to be said except Francis and Alex were still very curious as to why only the crabs were coming and going from the water.

"Francis, Alex, may I introduce Neva, one of my oldest friends?"

She pointed to this slightly odd looking piece of granite bouncing towards them. Francis extended his hand and received a warm and firm shake in return.

"Francis, heard lots about you."

"All bad, I hope."

"Well yes, most of it."

"Good! I knew I could trust her," Francis joked.

With both of them laughing the conversation went in one direction. Instant respect, you can't buy this luxury, it happens.

Gem seemed a little taken aback by this. Within a few moments Neva and Francis were slagging off everything in sight. Both of them seemed to possess no morals, forcing one another to outdo themselves in their rants as they looked about at their surroundings.

"Look at the state of your man!" or "Jesus, she needs to cover up!" they would say. At the bar, there were stones of every description. Neva was amazed by the knowledge Francis had regarding them. He raised his finger and started with Gem.

"Rhodonite, love the tiny, pink lines, very nice," winking at Neva. One by one he went through them all. "Jasper, don't know, don't know, basalt, limestone. Not too sure what that is but she's beautiful. Oh sorry, Neva you're . . . ?" Francis scratched his ear. "Wait, not granite." Francis was searching his mind when finally, shocked at his own brilliance, he shouted, "Obsidian!"

"You're going to do well here, Francis. Like father like son. He taught you well," Neva complimented him.

"I only know that because of the chips missing from your body, like the rock flint. Ancient tools would have been constructed from the same material of which you're made. My ancestors would have used it for everything from cutting up animals to weapons for hunting."

As they continued chatting Neva introduced everyone to Francis leading him around the locals one by one. For two days now, Francis had known Gem physically and her friends were treating him especially nice. He liked them instantly. It appeared they were having some sort of gathering, like a BBQ though without the burgers. Jesus this is so surreal! he thought. The only things missing are beach balls, deck chairs and lobsters. It looked like a bar on some Caribbean island. There were six massive tables of stone, each had some twenty small rocks acting as stools scattered around them. The bar had no beer taps like a pub, only water in large plastic glasses being filled by what looked like fresh water pumped up from some underground well.

"Oh my God, you have music?"

"Don't be too surprised Francis, the beach has adopted many great elements from your world, and a few . . . not so nice ones!" Neva replied. For a moment he thought about what the not so nice things could be. Neva started pulling him towards the bar.

"Hey Francis, what you want to drink?"

"Drink, you got drink also?" Francis was impressed.

"Well, we only drink water. Come to think of it we actually don't drink it; we toss it over one another. But there is always a case of beer under the counter if a wizard calls by."

"Oh yes, a cold beer would be fine. Could you get something for my sister also?"

"No worries," was the cheerful reply from Neva, as he searched behind the bar.

When Gem approached all he could do was peer straight into those sexy dark eyes. She knew he wanted to nibble on her like a chicken wing, exactly the way he had all week in his bed back in North Great George's Street. They hadn't even talked about that yet. In fact, she had said nothing, absolutely nothing!

Alex drank a small glass of beer in one swoop enjoying every drop by the expression on her face. Neva like all the other rocks on the beach looked dry as the sun was really hot. The heat must have spent years burning the surface of his skin if you could call it that Francis thought. With Gem and Alex standing beside them Neva raised his glass of water.

"Cheers, Francis. Alex, nice meeting you both."

Francis let the beer flow slowly into his mouth. Neva raised his glass above his head and tossed it all over himself. Alex was the first to crack up laughing followed by Francis. His mouth opened and released all the beer on top of Neva. Completely taken aback with embarrassment he tried frantically to wipe the beer from his rough chest. Alex was still laughing at the sight but Neva didn't seem to mind. He was gleaming.

"Relax, Francis. Cheers to you mate!"

Shaking his head in disgust at his actions, Francis couldn't have understood that Neva was cooling off. Gem then tilted her head backward and started pouring water over her head. It was at this moment that Francis turned to jelly for the first time in his life. The feeling was so strong that he nearly fell over. It took only a few moments for the hot sun to start drying her off, and he would have wished a lifetime imprisonment to watch the process over and over. If only he could have realised how real his dreams had become.

That day turned out to be one of the most enjoyable of summer. From start to finish he was so content to meet her friends, creatures, no stones or whatever they were, he thought. Over the course of the day, he drank the beers from behind the counter of *The Cock Tavern*, the name he christened it after finishing four bottles of the finest beer you would buy anywhere. It was then that Francis somehow felt that Gem, even as a stone, was part human, helped by the alcohol of course. But Alex also noticed. Neva saw it too but said something different to Francis.

"I never saw her so relaxed. She really seems at ease with you."

"Cheers, Neva. I like her too."

"You're both well crazy," Neva answered with a grin on his face.

More than you know, Francis thought.

Alex had spent the entire day chatting to everybody regarding this beautiful world. Francis was by now a little tipsy and distracted by his thoughts of seeing the headlines of the *News of the World*: "Son and daughter disappear in bathroom. Parents under investigation for murder. Basement excavated in search of bodies". He shook his head in a moment of despair, knowing they would soon have to return home. Thanking Neva for everything, he walked towards Gem.

"I should be heading home, you know I don't want to go."

"Francis, come later if you can."

Holding her around the waist gave him a sweet relaxing feeling. In fact he wasn't using his ears to their full potential. Francis was imagining kissing her lips; to him, the sensation resembled the first bite into a Choc Ice.

They talked for a while, they parted with a not-so-dry kiss and he knew that the chances of returning tonight were slim. All was good in his first relationship with a stone, he thought, walking off in search of Alex. When he found her, she was sitting directly behind a group of rocks having what appeared to be a discussion. She was fascinated with everything, except the conversation wasn't in English, so to suggest that she was lost would have been an understatement. He stood there for a while, a few steps back from Alex, and tried to take it all in. Ten seconds later, he tapped Alex on the shoulder.

"We should be going."

"Right, it will be about six at home." She looked at her watch.

The excitement of the last few hours and the fact that they had been sitting in the sun all day now showed. Like Francis, Alex was tired and wanted to eat dinner and go to bed early. Realising they could light the candle anywhere they moved away from the crowd and did so. Moments later they returned to the house on North Great George's Street. Upon arrival, Francis quickly blew out the small flame.

Within ten minutes of their return, Francis had taken a shower and brushed his teeth until his gums were bleeding in an attempt to hide the fact he had been drinking all day.

Later over dinner with their parents both of them had difficulty explaining their red faces since Dublin had been over cast for most of the day. Alex had said the beach was clear and that tomorrow they would be bringing sun block. Their mother suggested that they take their father's as there was some left over from his trip to Greece earlier in the year. Francis and Alex were now of the same mind regarding when it would be best to return to the beach. Though they hadn't discussed it yet both were thinking along the same lines. If the time difference was so close, as it seemed to be so far, they could go as often as they like; the best time being after lunch and again after their parents had fallen asleep. Neither of them seemed to care either way.

Lying in bed that night, Francis stared at the ceiling. "No stone, no stone," he repeated over and over. Everything with Gem appeared so natural. In the space of one week it was as if they had been going out a couple of months. Now he knew she was real. Everything before seemed like a dream, but it wasn't.

It had been five days since he got the stone and every night he had slept beside her with his wondering thoughts. Still lingering in the darkness of his mind was this question: *Why had they met? Was he falling in love and obsessed with her?* Really he had no idea what true love was, except she was always on his mind. Since touching the stone five days ago he thought of nothing else. Falling asleep that night he knew something was very different. *Yeah, I must be in love, he said to himself.*

Tossing and turning for what seemed ages, gradually he realised that sleep was not going to happen that night. Sometime after 3:00a.m., he went downstairs for a snack and made a small sandwich of bread and cheese. He poured a glass of water and started thinking. All he has done in the last few days is constantly see her in his mind, from the moment he woke, the very millisecond his subconscious closes those beautiful golden doors of his imagination. Which in Francis head were certainly two hundred feet tall? Her name popped into his head, and he felt great. He should have been really worried at this fact of obsession, but he wasn't.

"It's simple really. I'm missing something," he said aloud.

Dreaming, he stood there leaning against the kitchen counter, seeing himself in the middle of a green field surrounded by the most pleasant countryside. Above him were scattered cloud and the overwhelming sight of a woman who must have been as tall as the great pyramids. Gem was now a giant. She was enormous, which made her even sexier to Francis. Her hands waved above the top of the clouds as if she was walking in the middle of a field of wheat caressing their tops, like the wind as it passes over in a sweeping motion; her hands lowered, pushing through the clouds, and the air rushed between her fingertips. As she started to descend at great speed, her hair fell upwards.

Wearing his old jeans and a tight T-shirt, this creature of beauty was shrinking in size from what seemed like a thousand feet tall, to twenty feet, to five feet nine inches. Those dark eyes . . . those eyes were just slightly darker than his own, and he was drunk with them . . . so very drunk!

Chapter Ten

CRACKING UP

When Francis finally woke the next morning everything appeared normal. Of course, nothing would ever be normal in his life again, ever again! Once dressed, he headed down for breakfast feeling cheerful because he knew exactly what he was going to do. As soon as breakfast was over, he would be returning to the beach and upon arrival jump straight into bed with Gem.

Already a week into the summer holidays, Francis was now busy answering texts on his phone. He had read the first text shaking his head, then skipped to the last. It all proved too much so he put it down, unable to tell anybody what was really happening. Facing each other across the breakfast table, he and his sister were immersed in thought. It was plainly obvious they had very different intensions. Alex was so hyperactive her mother had wondered if she poured her daughter coffee instead of tea. Alex was desperate to inform the world of her fantastic adventures over the last few days. This was only normal considering what they had experienced. She was really struggling knowing she couldn't talk to anyone. Her mind was racing and unnaturally out of control. She had to talk to Eloïse today or else she would go completely mad!

After the second visit to the beach, the simple trick of stuffing their beds with yesterday's dirty clothes worked for a nocturnal trip. During the day, all they would say to their mother was that they were going to the beach. Francis looked at Alex across the table and knew that something was up. She was pale. In what looked like someone realising that they hate the food in their mouth she suddenly spat it out into the bowl laughing; there was nothing else she could do. The situation was too fantastic even to believe. They had travelled to another would, met talking crabs, had drinks with stones that had a human form of which some were as tall as a house. And the magic, God all the magic, Magic, MAGIC! She started laughing again with a wonderful giggle. Then slowly her expression began to change, her face narrowing as shock dawned on her and out came the words, *"Talking* crabs" after which her head fell straight into the bowl of cornflakes. SMASH!

Leaping from her seat, their mother screamed and instantly pulled Alex's head off the table. Francis jumped up and came round to help. Hoping she was only dizzy, he quickly ran a tea cloth under the tap and passed it to his mother who, in all fairness, was looking quite worried about her only daughter. After a few moments, all appeared well. Alex was awake and muttering all sorts of nonsense.

"Herman, he's a crab and has a big friend called Smasher."

Looking around lost for words, Francis began to laugh.

"She has such a great imagination!"

"Francis, who is she talking about?" their mother asked concernedly.

"I don't know, Mum."

Not wishing to take any chances their mother took Alex to the family doctor an hour later, where she had a long discussion regarding the health of her daughter. Alex fell asleep as the conversation was so boring. The doctor used this as an example,

"Alex is badly in need of fresh air."

When they returned home, Francis was instructed to watch over Alex while their mother went across town to run some errands. No sooner had she exited the house when the tone and atmosphere instantly changed.

"Jesus, Alex, what are you playing at? If Mum gets even a whiff of what we're up to it'll be the end," he shouted, glaring at her angrily.

"Why the fuck are you shouting at me like that? How long do you expect me to keep this crazy shit a secret?" She was shocked by his aggression.

Francis was starting to lose control and grew angrier at every passing moment.

"You better well find a way because nothing is stopping me from returning to the beach. Do you understand?" he yelled at her again.

Alex eyes started to swell. She was totally taken aback by this but also angry that Francis was not being more understanding about what was happening to both of them. Very upset, Alex ran from the house straight down the hill towards Eloïse's shop, and before she knew it was already in through the door jumping into the witch's arms.

It wasn't that Eloïse hadn't expected Alex but it was surprising that Alex knew she would be standing in front of the counter, facing the door. Alex needed to release all the feelings pent up inside of her and Eloïse was her only option. Crying at such a rate that Eloïse was concerned - even if she was aware of more than she let on - her huge, warm hug started Alex in the right direction.

"Now there dear girl, everything is going to be all right. Please come on around into the kitchen," her reassuring voice helped. "I will make you a cup of hot chocolate."

Alex began to show signs of recovery with her whole face relaxing in a sign of relief.

"You sit down and tell me all about it, Alex. All of it, my dear, from the very beginning."

Busily heating some milk on the stove, Eloïse added the powdered mix to the solid metal pot. Alex started chatting giving an instant impression she had a lot to discuss. The witch made sure the young girl received an extra portion.

Turning her head towards her, Eloïse said in a very understanding manner, "You had an argument with your brother, didn't you?" Alex looked up from the table slowly.

"Yes, we did, Eloïse. Why in God's name did you give us that candle?" she complained while still crying.

The wise old witch now faced away from Alex, hiding a huge grin of content on her face. For what seemed ages she said nothing, she only swirled the chocolate around and around with the wooden spoon.

"Alex, I did it because I care. No other reason. I have been around far too long, in human terms that is, nothing compared to the creatures on the beach, of course, but still long enough to know the power I possess used unwisely would be a waste, a total waste and an extremely bad end for all concerned. Please tell me more of what has happened."

Alex went straight into it, no holes barred. Eloïse listened to every word that was uttered from her young lips. She was like a Hoover sucking up every single bit of information, with no end in sight. Telling her all about the argument with her brother, within ten seconds, Alex had completely forgotten her shocking statement regarding the more disturbing intervention of Eloïse into the lives of herself and Francis by giving them the candle in the first place. For the moment, though, she was receiving all the mental stress attention that was required and, more importantly, it made her smile again. After all the excitement this girl had experienced since last Thursday Eloïse knew this was exactly what the doctor ordered.

"Your brother is growing up, Alex. What he's going through is completely normal for his age."

Placing the mugs of hot chocolate on the table, steam gushed up from them. Eloïse made herself comfortable and looked Alex straight in the eye.

"It's normal. He's growing up," she explained again.

"Yeah, you're right. To tell you the truth I don't blame him! She's so damn beautiful and nice. Have you ever seen a girl more perfect? She's a hottie - even if she's a stone." At this she suddenly burst out laughing.

"A stone indeed, Alex. One that holds a great amount of uncontrolled feeling inside her exactly like your brother, and who is experiencing the very same problems dealing with them."

Alex had long since stopped crying and now was deep in thought as Eloïse spoke. You could have accused Eloïse of casting some dark magical spell that had frozen Alex where she sat but she had done no such thing. All that was needed was the understanding of someone seeing two young people starting on a crazy adventure to another world and discovering that most people haven't a clue what's going on around them.

She couldn't believe how easy it was to talk to Eloïse. Of course, she was too young to understand it was made easy only for the facts of the last few days having no-one else to turn to for a nefarious reason. Alex mentioned they had seen many crabs on the beach but said nothing of having become friends with them, deciding that now probably would not be the best time, she planned to mention it on her next visit, all being well. Alex stayed for about an hour in the shop listening to Eloïse's advice; she found it very comfortable being able to get all her worries off her chest.

"Now remember you must talk to Francis immediately when you get home. Don't ignore him, and tell him you're feeling much better after chatting to me. Don't go into too much detail regarding what we were discussing but enough so he knows you understand his feelings," Eloïse suggested.

"Thanks, I was bursting to chat to someone. My mother would have my head examined if I were to tell her what's been happening the last few days."

With ease Eloïse placed her hand on Alex's head who then left glancing over her shoulder having no idea she was departing from the dragon's lair.

As soon as Alex entered through the back door of their house, Francis was waiting.

"Alex I'm sorry for shouting at you, really I am."

Alex walked over to him and gave him a soft hug.

"Yeah, I know you want to see Gem and that's cool," she released him, still holding his jumper.

Francis looked shocked for a moment, starting to relax once Alex explained she had only told Eloïse what she needed to know and nothing about the crabs and very little regarding Francis' relationship with Gem. In fact Eloïse did most of the talking she said, which put a smile on his face, as he wasn't prepared for her to know every detail of his involvement with a walking, talking stone.

"Eloïse is looking out for us both, Francis."

"So after lunch we'll go back to the beach," he suggested with delight.

"Together," she confirmed. Walking into the living room they both sat down to watch some television waiting for their mother to return.

It took Alex at least two minutes to convince her mum when she arrived, all was ok with herself and that Francis had agreed to take her out for some fresh air down to the beach.

The parting words from her daughter as she walked up the stairs to get ready "I'll be sixteen in three months," pounded in her mother's head like the distant drums from an old Tarzan movie. Run for your life and never look back as a thousand head-hunters were closing in for the kill.

"Are you ready, Francis?" Her impatience was clear.

"Oh yes, I am!" jumping off his bed.

Alex removed the candle from her shoulder bag and placed it on the small table at the end of his bed. Francis produced the lighter and lit it. Shortly afterwards, the ceiling gradually started to move. Shapes started to appear in the haze. The beginning of their return to the world that both of them were now completely obsessed with. From the ceiling the other world started dripping down the walls of his room like wet paint. Alex was gleaming with anticipation, similar to Francis. Breathing deeply, the fresh scent of the sea air started filling their lungs. A moment later they were surrounded by the other world, as Alex blew out the candle.

The sky was clear with a light breeze. They were not alone as they appeared beside a long line of rocks walking in the direction of the beach, being led by Herman who was giving orders waving his larger claw in all directions. The larger rocks were carrying wooden telegraph poles and huge amounts of construction materials, heading for the beach. "Hey good morning you two," he said, with what appeared to be a smile. They could sense he was truly surprised, maybe jealous that they possessed such power.

"Herman, what's happening?" they shouted back.

"Finishing off the building of the sets, for the games set to start later today."

"I might follow them Francis, do you mind?" Alex asked.

"Of course not . . . see you later, I'm going to stop by Gem's first," his voice was clear and he felt relaxed.

"I will take her with me Francis, and later I will explain the games ok!" Herman reassured him. Then he rushed off.

"No worries. See you both later."

Touching the bracelet around his wrist he knew he would find her on the beach. Both Eloïse and Herman had explained how they work. Francis trusted them like they were a television or mobile service you paid a monthly subscription to. *"You get what you pay for."* Of course Francis wasn't parting with any cash; he was on a freebie so it felt even better. It was strange but in front of him were three small cottages. Looking at the designs he guessed which one she was in. Having no doors, he walked in and saw her lying on a mattress with a cover over her. Kneeling down beside her without saying a word he saw her name in his mind.

"Gem?"

She turned around and looked up to him. She reached out to touch his face and feel his lips bringing him nearer for a kiss.

"Sweetie," she said smiling.

"And hello to you, girl," his answer was upbeat.

Francis had brought her a bottle of sparkling Irish spring water. This, he explained, was considered to be very refreshing. He pulled back the cover and began to pour it all over her body. It should be said that, at that moment, his red blood cells had no understanding of the message coming from his brain. She drank quietly because hot rocks do. In moments, that corner of the room resembled a sauna. Steam was rising from her body and lingering above their heads. By this time, Francis was under the covers rubbing his forehead into hers, moving his lips down to her eyes and softly kissing them. Moments later it appeared they had melted into each other.

They both lost track of time as it felt they had presumably spent hours lying beside each other. Francis started thinking of Alex. Gem suggested he go and look for her and she would come to find them later. Leaving the bed was more difficult than he imagined. Walking out the doorway, she called him back.

"Wait a moment," hers was the voice of a hypnotizing angel.

His eyes were focused on her head but his brain was scanning everything as she approached. She walked like a human, but her perfect shape would melt steel. She sprang forward with a quick step, wrapping her arms around him.

"You've such a soft touch."

"Oh shut up. *hold* me, Francis!"

At that moment, he knew she was half-stone and half-human, remembering when they first met her body was cold and lifeless to the world. Standing in her knickers and an old T-shirt of his, she held his face with her warm hands.

"Please take something from me to think about and don't forget me," she said.

"For sure. What?" he asked.

"Give me your wrist a moment."

Gem outstretched her arm and with her thumb and index finger on her left hand pinched her wrist. Little drops of what looked like water sparkled in the sunlight splashing onto the underside of his wrist.

She suggested he raise his arm to test the scent. My God, he thought, kissing her goodbye. He walked away, his mind racing after smelling her perfume on his wrist, he knew this would consume him all day like a virus unleashed upon this world that nothing could stop. He didn't understand what was happening. Right there and then, his brain and reason were not working in tandem.

The scent, all-powerful, beautiful, was relentless in its drive and motion. He thought of her essence as though it was something he could drink. Truly she had awoken him from a deep sleep. He floated across the lawn in front of the cottage.

Chapter Eleven

QUEST

Enjoying the walk towards the beach, which took a few moments to reach, he paused to look at the flat outstretched area of sand before him. It was incredible, the very moment he placed his foot on the sand about thirty feet away what resembled a mole hill popped up followed soon after by another. Their heads didn't turn. Those eyes spun around to face any direction. He started crossing this small stretch of flat sand known as the dead zone. It wasn't that Francis was afraid. Yesterday, Gem had explained the existence of the creatures trapped within the sand. Each grain of sand might be from one creature, and only together can they make this shape or form. Six of them now followed at a distance, staring with those huge, hollow eyes.

Last time there had been a handful, but today they were popping up everywhere. Looking back, they moved faster and faster towards him.

"Oh no, they didn't do that yesterday!" he said now slightly worried.

Reaching the other side, he jumped onto the solid ground and turned back to watch. They were climbing over each other to reach him. They arrived at the edge like a wave breaking around his feet on a beach. Why would they do that he thought? The difference on this occasion being that the sand did not return to the dead zone. It stopped there, not moving. Looking down he could see large, gaping eyes. They appeared so sad. But that's not what moved him. They were looking to Francis, as if for sympathy. What could he do, though, to help these dead souls? Quietly fading into nothing, they lay still on the hard rock.

Shaking the sand from his feet, he took a few steps backwards before turning around and continuing on his way. Still holding the image in his mind, he found the pure wonderment of it all a little overpowering. His eyes were moist. Surprisingly, though, he wasn't afraid. All he wanted was to understand them - they didn't appear dangerous - but how could he do that being new to this world. Francis simply didn't understand how to go about things. It was like one of the thousands of daydreams he had at school that got him into so much trouble. Making it up as you go along, fixing all that needed to be changed so that everything was right in his world was easy given that he was in control most of the time.

However, this wasn't a daydream. He was actually here. So, for the moment, he walked on in search of Alex. Herman had said that it would never be a problem, that the magical bracelet would lead him to her and other friends on the beach. Putting his trust in this, he followed his nose until she came running towards him very excited. She crashed into him screaming and out of breath.

"Francis! I was chatting to a piece of limestone! He's down there with Herman now waiting for us."

Pausing again to catch her breath, she pointed in a very general direction. "He told me this crazy story about a piece of sandstone that knows everything, and has been around forever. Remember Eloïse mentioned something about him in the shop?"

"Yeah, I do remember something about that, alright."

"This limestone guy said he met a small piece of granite, meant to be a cousin or something from the other one, and this guy was always telling this story about some bloke called Jesus."

"Jesus?" he answered.

"Yes, Jesus Christ, Francis."

"Jesus Christ, for real?" Now he looked shocked.

"Yes, that's what I've been trying to tell you," she insisted.

"Jesus, that's nuts!"

"Francis, stop saying that, I am deadly serious about this," she was starting to get extremely angry.

"Oh my God."

"FRANCIS!" she screamed at the top of her voice.

"What?"

Realising what was happening he started laughing followed by Alex.

"It's crazy we might actually be able to meet someone who has talked to Jesus," she said.

For a moment Francis stood there thinking about the massive implications it would have for his mother if she found out; she attended mass almost every week.

"Sorry Alex, you mean, of course, someone who possibly hit Jesus in the head as he was being stoned, or was alone in a field as he walked past. Sadder still, he could have watched his last moments on the hill called Golgatha."

"It's so crazy, so utterly mad" he said.

"I know. Imagine it," she gleamed. Seeing her face made Francis very happy as she was so excited, so full of life, as he pushed her forward in the direction she had come running. For such a glorious sunny day there seemed nothing better to do than to help his sister search for the stone that may have hit Jesus in the head. And with such a great guide as Herman to assist they might actually do it, he thought. Think of the story! They would know the truth. There must have been fifty billion stones on this beach; it looked like an inhabited planet in the Milky Way Galaxy.

After walking a short distance they found Herman sitting on top of a stone. He was having a conversation with a small lump of quartz which looked so absolutely beautiful, Francis found it extremely difficult to concentrate, and started squinting while seeing stars. He looked down at Alex and was about to speak when suddenly he had forgotten what he was going to say and turned back to the quartz once more. No matter what came into his head, he couldn't say anything, so hypnotised was he by this little shining object. He turned away, because he sensed something was wrong: not harmful, irresistible. This piece of quartz was a living firework that was exploding and crackling with every word it spoke, its lips rubbed together and sparks went a-flying, like a tiny volcano spitting out its lava. It was a sight to behold. Alex seemed in agreement. She was very quiet.

"Herman," Francis said aloud, still staring at the quartz.

"Francis, Alex, come nearer please I want you to meet someone. I have been talking to this delightful piece of quartz and she has told me something that might be of great interest to you. . . regarding the stone you're looking for."

"What, wow. Please go on."

Francis was now completely spellbound by the piece of quartz. They both failed to notice the look on Herman's face. Although it was hard to judge what a crab was thinking but Herman's eyes went to heaven and started tapping two of his claws together. He knew that Francis and Alex were both under the spell of the quartz. After a moment or two this sparkling beauty's fire seemed slightly duller to them both.

Herman quickly explained to them that the quartz was hypnotising them though they were unaware it had affected them so powerfully. Actually, it turned out that she was pleased they liked her and that was the reason she was giving off more light than normal, and didn't even notice it herself. She spoke a strange language that Herman seemed to understand with ease.

"You're a Rose Quartz aren't you?" Francis said with profound happiness. He was showing off his knowledge of geology.

Followed by a moment of silence, after which Herman started to translate. Turning to Francis, her lips started clattering as they moved over each other creating sparks. Tiny firecrackers were exploding from her mouth. Herman quickly moved backwards to avoid one of the sparks that shone brightly, and then vanished in a tiny puff of black smoke. Alex managed to take out her digital camera.

"Shit, why didn't I bring mine? Damn!" Francis had forgotten it again.

"Alex, take one of Herman. No wait, better still get them both in if you move back a bit."

"Francis, Alex, may I introduce you both?" Herman waited till they both had his attention. "She has seen a great many things on this earth and well she's friendly and willing to speak freely to us about almost anything, in fact she confirmed what I thought . . . we need to find Sandstone or a piece of him who met your friend Jesus."

"A piece of him." Francis was overjoyed at his own words.

Herman started tapping his feet together again and the clattering of his rings sounded like a song of sorts ringing out across the beach. Francis looked at Alex. She shrugged her shoulders in reply. Then an answer came over the soft breeze. A confident crab appeared over the top of a large rock directly to the right of them. It was a solider crab. He moved forward ever so slightly and precisely as Francis was about to speak he sped off down the rock moving with great speed and agility. Circling behind Alex, he jumped between her feet, leaped across the narrow path and dashed over the smaller rocks. All three of them stood motionless. Peering from tiny, beady eyes you could tell something was different about him. And then he was off again.

Herman was completely fed up with his antics and tossed his claws in the air, shouting.

"Eric it's ok. Slow down! I told you that we are assisting some guests and I don't want you milling around. Please come over and introduce yourself to Francis and Alex."

"Ok!" came the snappy reply. With that, he crept towards them. Almost looking like he was stalking his prey before closing in for the kill, his legs moving in slow motion, the tips of his feet etched into the stone like ice picks, and he left no marks as he moved onto the sand. Alex took a step backwards from this tiny forbidding creature.

"ERIC!" Herman screamed.

"Sorry. Lieutenant Ericson at your service."

Alex was still a little apprehensive, and Francis had to admit that Eric being barely twice the size of a golf ball totally put him on edge. His feet touched the ground like strong, German-made kitchen knives picking at the stone, resembling some ancient stone mason's tools reserved for the finest detail in a masterpiece of sculpture.

Francis and Alex introduced themselves as Herman told him what they were looking for. This little crab was very eager to help. He kept going on about how successful his unit was and how proud he was of the crabs under his command which made what happened next so strange. Eric, although a little intimidating at first glance, was definitely a creature of trust. It was remarkable that after such a sinister display, Francis found himself walking towards him with open eyes and instantly they were best friends, at least from Francis's point of view.

Of course, he was impressed by Eric, but who wouldn't be? Eric had all the craziness Francis wanted, respected and admired. His father was similar in some ways but Eric was ridiculous in the extreme. Everything about him deserved respect. His outer shell was glistening an ocean blue from the midday sun and changed ever so slightly as he moved, almost like a chameleon. One of his eyes pointed towards Herman, the other was on Francis and Alex.

"Happy to assist you both," he said in a clear English accent.

"This is my younger sister, Alex, and we are visitors from Dublin. Sorry, actually I'm not so sure about that . . . I mean I'm not too sure where this is. I know we are from Earth and we are both very happy to be visiting this wonderful place you live in," he said beaming from one side of his mouth to the other.

Instantly thousands of eyes peaked over the stones surrounding them, revealing an army of crabs.

"Why, thank you for being so honest. Inform me what we can do for you," he asked lifting his left claw into the air while turning to greet his soldiers.

Herman started telling Eric about Eloïse and the candle, which he also seemed very surprised that they had in their possession. He knew the object was of great value.

After all three of them had discussed their travels, Francis mentioned they were searching for a stone that hit a human in the head over two thousand years ago.

"We heard Sandstone might know something and be able to help."

"Ok . . . let me get this straight. You want me to ask the west sea brigade, which I command, to search for a stone that hit some bloke over two thousand years ago. Hmmmnnn. What's his name again?"

"Ehh yes . . . Jesus," Francis confirmed.

"Jesus hey . . . what does he look like?"

Herman, Francis and Alex looked at each other puzzled until Alex said, "I think he would have been around thirty years old, tall with a beard, and probably looked like he lived on a beach for most of his life."

"Sorry, I meant the stone," Eric explained.

"Oh! We know it's a piece of sandstone Eric, that's all," she said.

"Ok . . . I see your problem. Sandstone is, as you may have realised, everywhere on the beach."

As he said this, a massive piece of sandstone the size of a car walked past sending everyone running to give it room.

Francis' thoughts drifted for a moment. Here we are surrounded by thousands of talking crabs. Chatting away like grannies in a coffee shop. For a second he remembered what Eloïse had said. *Don't talk to the crabs.* Looking about he shook his head . . . they are very friendly, and well Herman is fantastic. This short daydream was abruptly ended by a crab.

"Let's head further down the beach. I need to sort out some details regarding the games," suggested Herman.

Eric gave the orders and suddenly all the crabs starting moving like a carpet over the rocks. In moments, they had all vanished. Francis and Alex started walking ahead of Herman who let them do so.

Standing alone he shook one of his legs and a ring dropped to the ground. The slow movement of his tiny eyes from left to right would have seemed a little worrying to Francis and Alex had they seen it and even more so had they understood the reason. Herman felt worried. Like something needed his immediate attention. That sense of impending disaster of five hundred years ago when Gem was last on the beach had suddenly returned. He needed to be absolutely sure, have no question or doubt. He left the ring were it lay and quickly returned to the others. As he ran, you could hear his rings clattering together. It sounded almost like words in a message drifting across the beach to Smasher.

As the group moved away over the top of a small sand dune, the ring still lay flat on the ground. It reflected the sunlight as only a precious metal can. Directly beside it was a small cave. There was nothing strange about it. Thousands of them were scattered about the beach. Mostly, the crabs used them to cool off on very hot days. This one had a creature inside hidden within the shadow of the entrance. Even to the trained eye of the solider crab it would be completely invisible. If you were to spare a moment and peer inside the entrance you might see something of interest, but most certainly you wouldn't see a crab.

Another massive creature strolled past the entrance and a number of smaller rocks fell from the sidewall, rolling towards the bottom. But one stone kept on falling after the others had long stopped. Bumping into smaller ones of every description it changed direction like it was a tumbling drunk on O'Connell Street in the capital of Ireland. But it didn't do what you would expect from a normal stone as it stopped abruptly beside the ring. Then for a moment in its reflection the beauty of the sun's rays exposed the true face within the stone.

Disguised as a normal rock, invisible to all, stood a four inch long, black crab. It had a nasty, protruding scar that cut deep into its forehead running between its jet black eyes. It picked up a small pebble from the ground. The magic protecting it shimmered left to right like the image on an old television after you whack the side of it with your hand in an attempt to improve the reception. Revealed for a brief moment were its legs covered in rings of every description.

It raised its claw above the ring and paused before dropping the tiny pebble into its centre, whereupon it suddenly like the ring disappeared in a minute flash of light. After which the stone simply rolled away.

Chapter Twelve

BAD MEMORIES

Inside his house, alone in near darkness, Smasher waited, crouching on one knee; his right fist was held high above his head, visible by the small amount of light provided through the little window; his movement noticeable due to the dust falling from his muscles grinding together; his eyes were focused on a crude circle drawn on the floor with white chalk. Sounds could be heard from outside the building but he continued to stare at this spot, sensing that something was about to happen. It started with a humming noise and a tiny sparkle of light that formed above the circle on the floor. Smasher's eyes squinted with clear anger as the dot of light grew in size. A second later it had disappeared.

Together Herman's ring and a pebble appeared, falling a few inches to the floor. Smasher let the full force of his powerful fist pulverise the spot instantly. He was so fast his fist reached them before they hit the ground. Quickly raising his arm again, he rammed his fist into the floor for a second time. The force with such strength his fist went through the floor a foot or two as dust flew into the air around the room. Waiting till it had settled before he dared take a look. As he had expected to see something else, his disappointment was clear; but for the dust only Herman's ring was there. No sign of a crab, a terrible, black crab.

Again, Smasher rammed the floor to vent his anger. He knew it to be no accident that Herman and he had felt the presence of an old enemy after the arrival of Gem with Francis and Alex on the beach. Lost in thought, he stared at the floor. Smasher understood far too well that if this evil crab was back on the beach it was terrible news. The last time they faced him, Herman and Smasher had nearly lost everything. Smasher stretched out his hand and the little ring, undamaged, sprang from the ground and stuck fast to the top of his index finger. For a five tonne rock, he walked briskly out the door, in the direction of the beach to find Herman.

Francis, Alex and Herman walked towards the centre of the beach. The small pathway they were on had opened up once past the dunes. They now had a great view of the surrounding area. A few hundred metres to the left was the water's edge which pushed up a light, cool breeze considering how hot it was for midday. Herman stopped and looked about.

"Here is as good as anyplace you two. Sit down, please."

"Thanks Herman," Francis said eagerly.

He sat down beside Alex who had dropped to the ground the fastest. Herman smiled at her enthusiasm, but secretly wished he had better tidings to share with them both.

"So, you two kind-hearted souls . . . from the beginning I suppose. Gem has lived on this beach three times before, this being the fourth during the past few thousand years. At the end of the first two times she left of her own accord. The third time she was trapped as a stone Francis, the way you brought her on this occasion. The difference being that she was not released last time but used and abused by an extremely nasty crab. He found a way of keeping her as a stone and using her power for himself. Basically, she loved him and he used her. That's why you might have some problems understanding her in the next few days Francis. She lived passed the point of no return. And when I look at her now, I see that she is so happy because you don't take anything from her."

"Well, yeah," Francis acknowledged.

"Yes Francis, but you should understand that won't last forever. The last time she was here, she lost everything she ever wanted. The reason she is ok now is because she is carrying around a part of you within herself. Your best part . . . and that link will break. She is sheltering you from part of her life because she wants to protect herself, so she won't make the same mistakes again."

Francis was searching for words because he felt unsettled.

"I know you're being nice to warn me of all that Herman," he replied.

"Francis, I have to because nobody else will. Every human who has ever come here is special. I mean they are witches, wizards or a heavy-hitting sorceress. You two have something but I don't know what that is because it's all a little strange you arriving with the candle and Gem in your pocket."

Realising that Francis had had enough of this conversation, Alex tried to change the subject. "Will she play in the games?"

"Well, I am afraid the news doesn't get any better. I might as well be straight up front. The games are recklessly dangerous for all involved," he replied.

"How dangerous, Herman?" Francis asked, looking straight down at the crab.

Although uneasy about discussing his relationship with Gem, Francis was not upset, slightly unsettled perhaps but he may have run before he could walk. From Herman's point of view, it looked like a dam had burst, with a river having been locked from its natural course now finally free to make its wonderful journey towards the sea.

"Herman, I mean I have been in love before. Well, maybe not love, but I have loved." Francis paused because he knew he couldn't answer that question the way he wanted to; he was unfortunately too young and lacking the correct experience.

"It always ends in tears," he continued smiling.

Herman was reacting to this news with the same understanding that Eloïse had shown Alex in the shop yesterday and that's all that mattered.

"Maybe you will share that maybe you won't. Life is about living the moment. Believe me, I have been around long enough."

After an awkward pause, Herman tried to distract them both by telling more stories about the games. Regrettably that got him into even worse trouble as the news would surely be more distressing.

"Hey, don't stop now Herman! I need to know everything."
Francis was beside himself with excitement.

"Well, the larger stones, Smasher for example, play ball
games similar to your rugby and suchlike. All you need to
do is stay well out of the way. There are also hiding games
where our beach mixes with your world. As people walk
along the beach they can, for a moment, pick up the stones
and creatures from here, and if these creatures are thrown
into the ocean we won't be seeing them for a very long time.
You know this beach is covered in magic, right? It's used
by every creature for every reason, but that still won't help
you if you're a stone. Crabs are born of the sea so we can
move freely in and out. Like yourself. As a human you have
a natural connection with water. We're the only ones able
to enter the water and return. If a stone is thrown into the
sea it must wait to be returned naturally as it will have no
other means. Their magic won't work in the water, and the
crabs don't interfere with such things anymore as in the past
it has caused so much stress and unwanted disturbance for
everyone. Only on a few rare occasions have stones walked
from the sea unhindered. For that is the way of nature. Even
though Gem has taken human form, because of you Francis,
this will change nothing. If she goes into the sea, it is the
end. It could take hundreds of years for her to return by
natural means. No magic in this world will bring her back."

On hearing this, Francis grew worried. Alex placed her hand
on his shoulder and rubbed it softly. Looking for some hope, he
stood up smiling at Alex.

"Well, it's not as if we're finished. We are kind of crazy about
each other, and I'm certainly not going to damage that." His
reply was passionate.

"Great, finally I got that off my chest, as you humans say!"
Seizing the moment, Herman jumped in the air, shouting.

Alex laughed and Francis also saw the lighter side things.
They had an unspoken understanding that this conversation
was for their ears only.

"Excellent!!! Let's move on," Herman commanded.

That's when Alex saw something that Francis had missed as; again, he was lost in thought. It was a tiny glint, possibly the smallest mannerism you could recognise but she saw it on Herman's face. He was holding something back. As she ran to catch up with the others, Alex didn't understand what this all meant. By the time she had reached them, she had forgotten even what she had seen. Let alone thought!

Stretching out for miles, the beach was teaming with life. Millions of creatures were roaming about; some had formed columns marching across the centre in all directions. Down near the sea, a building which looked like a platform and catapult was being constructed. Francis and Alex were amazed. At the back of the beach, built into the cliff face was a massive football stand with literally thousands of creatures. Every shape, colour and size gazing towards the centre of the beach, where most of the games were to be played. They were like an army of stone. Francis started naming them, as easy as when his father had returned from a trip to some coal, silver or diamond mine in Africa and opened his suitcase packed full of strange rocks. There were simply too many so he stopped describing them.

"It's beautiful," Alex exclaimed, as she took another shot from the camera.

"Listen, I could recognise that sound anywhere," Herman admitted from below.

To Francis and Alex it sounded like a rumble. They turned around to see a huge piece of stone rushing towards them.

"Smasher!" Herman shouted. By this time he had slowed to a mere walking pace, but you could feel how powerful he was. He didn't waste any time and got straight to business by dropping the ring beside Herman. In his very deep tone of voice, he said, "I guess José's back from the deep."

"Damn! *Damn!* **Damn!**" yelled Herman. He started walking in circles. "Smasher, I told them everything about Gem's history."

At that moment, Smasher's old face said everything to Francis. You could have read the word *dread* from his expression.

"Francis, this changes everything. I will tell Gem and all others who need to know. José is ruthless, he destroyed two of my friends, tortured Gem for years and banished lots of good rocks to the bottom of the ocean, from which only one has returned, to this day." He pointed to Smasher.

"If I see him, he's dead!" Herman screamed.

Smasher started muttering and was growing angrier by every word. Herman tried to calm him down.

"My good friend, you will get the chance." Francis felt the emotion from Smasher. "Wait a moment, Herman please," Francis raised his voice. "Smasher, I understand. I would enjoy seeing you smash him. I will do ANYTHING to protect Gem."

Reacting to the flow of emotion from Francis, Smasher became even angrier. Like he was reading the thoughts of Francis and he liked it. For all present, it was very unnerving to see.

"Hold on a moment you two," Herman shouted.

But it was too late. Somehow, Smasher was feeding off the emotions of Francis. Francis wanted to smash his fists into the ground. A moment later, Smasher did exactly that with his fists. The result being two large holes in the sand and a lot of dust tossed into the air. Everyone looked at Francis. Herman was visibly taken aback.

"So we have come to it at last, Francis. You're able to channel your feelings into others, or from others. It doesn't surprise me now. It's taken a few days but I guessed that you had been experiencing something strange."

"You're right, Herman," Alex broke in. "Something happened to me also. I have always been able to tell if someone is near, or something is about to happen. But since we arrived I've noticed things I don't understand, the slightest change in people's behaviour."

Francis tried to apologise to Smasher. "That's crazy, Smasher. Are you ok? I was angry also and wanted to show you I would help. I didn't mean to cause you any harm. Not that I could anyway you're so strong. But I felt I had control over your body. That was so strange,"

Herman now saw Francis as though he was a giant in the shadow of another giant similar to Smasher.

"It seems you two have much more going on than we first suspected. I mean you arrive with Gem, followed by the number one evil crab of all time, José, and both of you start changing into I don't know what. Alex is seeing into the future and, Francis, you're a train wreck about to happen. That's it. I've had it up to here! Someone is moving things around us. It's too great a coincidence."

They all looked at each other. Together, they realised that Eloïse had to be the answer. With the manners of a gentleman, Herman requested to know more about how they got here with the candle. Any details overlooked in their last conversation might shed some light on the strange circumstances regarding their journey to this altered world.

"Hold on a moment everyone; let's not burn the witch at the stake yet! Eloïse is a lovely woman. I don't know too much about her but I can't imagine all that you're thinking is true. All she did was encourage us and she advised us both to see what happens," Francis stressed.

"Go with the flow," Alex recalled.

"Francis, Alex the fact is that you have some hidden abilities, now pushing their way to the forefront. It's completely unbelievable that Eloïse has nothing to do with what's happening. I have to question that." Herman said,

"Well, it's true she gave us the stone. You're saying that she knew José would return from the sea? But why would she want me and José to even meet. How could I change anything?"

"Francis, all I know is that you and your sister are changing every moment you stand on this beach," Herman admitted that's what he understood from everything.

Gradually they all started moving again. It must be said, though, that some tension was in the air leading to one conclusion regarding Eloïse.

Unable to have any speedy verbal conversation in English, slowly Smasher informed Francis of all the ways he had tried to kill José the last time they had seen each other and also how Herman had given him a terrible scar across his forehead in battle. Smasher had ripped out an entire section of the main stand as José ran for his life. In the end Herman had tried to cut him in half, but José had protected himself by turning into a stone and that's the shape they left him in when they tossed him back into the sea all those years ago. Since then, they had heard nothing from him. In fact, they were certain he would never be seen again as the majority of his magical ability was destroyed.

Besides this, Alex was telling Herman all she knew regarding Eloïse. Insisting that she was good, she believed that if she knew what was happening she would assist in any way that she could. Herman listened to the whole story that Francis and Alex had withheld from Smasher and himself because they didn't want to tell everybody where and how they had arrived on the beach. Alex found it a little awkward but remembered to leave out all the untrusting stories regarding crabs that Eloïse had confided in them, but at the same time convinced him that they were well-informed about the creatures living here.

Herman was intrigued by this wizard. He told them both he had seen everyone who had visited the beach. He felt that he should have remembered her but couldn't and it puzzled him to no end. Hence all the questions from which Alex was starting to tire. Similarly, Francis had had enough. He explained that he was off to find Gem and would catch them later. Chatting, the others went on down the beach into the distance.

It took Francis a while to find Gem but it was made all the easier by using his bracelet. It got brighter the nearer you got to the person for whom you were looking. Francis was nearly running as the excitement was brewing inside him: the tingly feeling you get from obsessive madness. All the events of the last few hours were on the tip of his tongue. Like a child running to his mother he was ready to jump into her arms. Gem was sitting in The Cock Tavern around a table of solid stone; similar in size to the one Smasher had tried to flatten José with, in the past. There were some others with her and it had the feeling of a Sunday afternoon down the pub.

Before he reached her, one of the creatures signalled that he was approaching and she started to turn around. Seeing only the back of her head excited him; strands of her hair caught the light breeze. The sun was behind her so her face was in shadow. Light shot out from all around her head in every direction like shooting stars in the night sky.

Sadly the peach he had licked was rotten. Up until thirty minutes ago, he had never really thought about such rottenness. A spell! Only now was he aware of it. Seeing it for the first time was like looking into a fire that would go out if you didn't toss more wood on. She wanted it this way and it was her choice. She was making the move, the end of the game.

"I'm with my friends, Francis. See you tomorrow."

Everyone at the table turned around for a moment and then returned to their business, realising the conversation was not intended for them. Francis felt embarrassed, but held his control as best he could.

"Ok. I wanted to see how you are. What's up?" he inquired.

"Francis, what's up is I'm with my friends so leave me alone." She turned away from him.

For a long moment, he stood there in complete shock.

"What the hell's going on?"

She didn't answered him so he left, not prepared to take that sort of treatment from anyone. As he walked from The Cock Tavern, he paused twice, thinking about returning to find out what was happening. He was now enraged. Stones could be so hard, but stony girls!

Chapter Thirteen

TRUE COLOURS

With all the noise and commotion on the beach it was easy to understand that nobody would notice a few small pebbles being knocked over by an invisible creature as it crawled about listening to the conversations of whomever it wanted without their knowledge. This creature climbed atop a small mound of pebbles about two feet high. A number of stones tumbled to the base as a little hollow appeared to be dug out from the top. When finished, it looked like a duck was sitting down on its nest of tiny hatchlings. The difference being you couldn't see the creature, apart from the hollowed-out depression. Spreading its body out it knocked a few more pebbles down the side. However this wasn't a duck. It was José sitting about twenty feet from Alex who was totally unaware that her entire conversation with a lovely piece of basalt was being listened to by the most evil crab ever to crawl from the sea.

Down the beach, Herman and Smasher were deep in thought regarding the arrival of José, for he would surely seek revenge on both of them no matter what happened. This meant that many creatures would be injured or killed. If his goal was to take Gem it would be a disaster for all concerned and they both knew it. Herman was asking Smasher about being controlled by Francis. Smasher didn't seem to mind.

"It was what I wanted anyway. Smash my fist into the ground pulverising everything," Francis explained.

They glanced at each other.

"Yeah I like both of them too, Smasher, he reminds me of you a little, old friend, but honestly what the hell is going on? Two humans suddenly arrive on the beach with a transport candle while having no understanding of how valuable it is."

"Wait for it! Apparently, given to them by a witch who said 'go have some fun and see what happens'. Yeah right, am I meant to believe that?"

Smasher had a moment to smile as Herman stopped talking. He knew it would be better to let him continue ranting as it helped him think straight.

"Also what's with them both? I know Francis is young in human terms, but he has such deep raw emotion I can't put my claws on. Alex sees the finest details and feels when something is about to happen and she's getting better at it. Oh, and did I mention Gem's back with them both? Followed by the master of misery, José."

Smasher raising his closed fist to his mouth coughed aloud as he wanted to say something. Herman quickly intervened by walking forward and shouting up to Smasher's head some ten feet above.

"Hey, they're bloody looking for sandstone as well!"

"Sandstone, how did they find out about sandstone?" Smasher asked.

"Alex has been talking to everyone and found someone who talked too much. So now I am playing along," Herman replied.

"Well, it would be nice to see him again," Smasher's voice was soft.

"You and me both, my friend, but not because he hit some guy, Jesus, two thousand years ago doesn't mean we have to introduce them." Herman went silent. He appeared shocked.

"Jesus, did Sandstone ever mention that name to you?" he asked Smasher who shook his head in a no gesture.

"I solemnly believe they have good intentions, Smasher. They knew nothing of our beach before last week. I'm sure they're searching for him because of his connection with their world in the past, that's all. Maybe someone is using Francis and Alex to reach Sandstone because they can't find him. They wouldn't even comprehend they are being used. That's the way they want it to be, the person - or creature - behind this whole mess. We are smack in the middle of some grand design and have no control over the matter. We must take control, twist it, help it along and bring the other party out into the light."

Eric was racing along the beach at top speed followed by his two most trusted lieutenants. When he reached Herman and Smasher it was obvious from his expression that something was up. Gone was the show-off and contemptuous behaviour.

"Herman something terrible has happened beside the main catapult. Please come with me NOW."

Smasher quickly placed his hand on the sand. Herman, Eric and both his lieutenants climbed on. Eric attempted to explain, as Smasher took giant leaps along the beach towards the catapult which was beside the shoreline about a mile away. Everyone scrambled to avoid him. Even for his massive size Smasher was extremely agile, weaving in and out of the crowd, avoiding contact with the larger creatures and trying to jump over the smaller ones unable to move out of his way fast enough. Eric began the grim task of informing Herman what had happened. Seconds later the massive hulk of stone came to an abrupt stop at the base of the platform supporting a catapult of sorts to be used in the games.

Smasher's giant hand opened, lowering gently to the ground. At first Herman's eyes were visible from the centre of his stony palm. They blinked once. Coming forward with the others Herman started to curse under his breath at the sight awaiting him. On the sand lay three dead crabs beside one of the giant wooden pillars supporting the platform. They were jet-black having been burnt by powerful magic. Two were adult spider crabs and the third a young beach crab. Smasher was grinding his teeth. It was a terrible sight to behold as the last moments of their lives were frozen. The pain in their appearance was a sign of their horrible death. The silver rings on all their legs were unmarked. The younger crab that possessed a very small skinny ring was holding it before his face in what looked like a cry for help.

Herman was incensed by this scene. He quickly told the others to bring the charred remains to him as he dropped a ring to the ground from one of his legs. When all three bodies were beside it while controlling his deep emotions; under his breath whispered some words and they vanished. By this time, a sizeable crowd had gathered to investigate what all the commotion was about with a number of soldier crabs keeping them at a distance. Herman knew it was better to inform the whole beach now, and try and save some lives. Walking around in circles he wished for nothing but to kill José right now, this very second. He paused controlling himself. Screaming and shouting would only alarm everyone and give José what he wanted.

"Eric, please quietly inform every creature on the beach that José is back."

As Eric left with his men, Herman paced back and forth under Smasher's shadow.

"That bastard is going to pay for this Smasher, you hear me."

"Oh, I do," rumbled the giant rock.

They both walked around to the front of the platform and stared ahead to the awesome sight of the natural Grandstand of the Cliff, about a mile away in the distance filled to the brim with thousands of creatures. Between them and the stand there was a vast area of sand and shell with thousands of creatures scattered about, busy with their business. And of course the few scattered islands of sand dunes full of creatures who had no intention of leaving knowing they had the best view of the games, being smack in the centre of them.

The platform was now crowded with all the heads of every organisation that existed on the beach. Dazzling, fantastic looking, this event definitely was. Considering the games were taken from mankind's history and its ways of celebration, it was peculiar it had none of the normal human-like decoration. It didn't need any bunting, balloons or marching bands. Being present, witnessing was enough. All the creatures partaking were present before the platform. Herman and Smasher had walked over to the other competitors. Every size, shape and type was represented. There was even a tiny walnut star crystal.

It was one of only two ever seen on earth. The other one had fallen from the heavens thousands of years ago when trapped by the earth's gravity. It was indestructible.

When discovered first, it had emitted light for over two hundred years because of the heat absorbed from re-entry through the atmosphere. When word spread across the Persian empire of the time, it was judged too valuable for any one country and so it was decided to hide it forever. It was placed in the centre of a statue that now rests, unknown to all, in the National Museum of Iran, in Tehran.

The other walnut star crystal standing beside Smasher was about one foot tall and badly in need of a wash. It was surrounded by a number of smaller crabs that liked the look of it. Their rings sparkled in the hot sun, over-polished for the opening ceremonies. Herman had been joined by Alex and Francis and all now stood together, away from the contestants. Gem was not present at the opening.

Then, without warning, the grand master of ceremonies stepped forward.

"Enjoy!" he shouted and rang a great bell on the stage for all to hear.

Thousands of creatures shouted with joy for they knew the games could commence. Herman took Alex and Francis back to The Cock Tavern. Francis felt every footfall he placed on the sand; looking back he saw them as marks leading him away from Gem. He desperately needed to talk to her; the manner and directness of their last meeting had scared him.

Dreaming of things passed and matters he wanted to discuss with her had given him the appearance of a person under stress. To Francis it was obvious that Gem wanted to deny him a chance to stay friends and be normal. Slowly, this was eating away at his feeling and was exactly how it appeared to anyone observing him. He looked drained, tired, but secretly all he was doing was hiding his anger at how she could be so harsh with him. Like dimming a light in an already badly-lit room. Something had to give. Francis' brain knew all too well what was going on but had no control. He guessed it was her way of trying to finish things. But why?

They had spent the last six months having a fantastic relationship under the spell. Of course, Francis had only met her a week ago. Love (lust) is one of the very few reasons for someone's brain to shut down, but that's normal, he was human. He was obsessed and definitely at the centre of a falling star. His heart was ruling now and reason was like a fading memory. Pure emotion was taking over; it pulsated inside him and all around could feel something. But it wasn't like he had magical powers. Firstly he had no rings and wasn't trained as a wizard. But every creature that came near him sensed a difference like a feeling you get at the tip of your tongue when searching for the correct word in an important conversation that your life depended on. But no one could explain it. Francis was changing.

When they arrived at The Cock Tavern, it appeared another party was happening, with loud music and everyone chatting. There was an old human wizard dancing in front of a group of younger witches who appeared to be having a hen party. It was a welcome distraction for Francis as they were all in bikinis. Even in Dublin you wouldn't see that. For a second Francis stretched his body and tilted his head to heaven smiling.

Their home in Dublin on the first floor had two small balconies looking down to hundreds of partygoers from the north side of the river heading into town. Many Friday nights had been spent with friends watching hordes of women going off into the city looking for adventure with most of their clothes missing.

Neva saw him coming and gave a shout to join him at the bar. It took only a moment before a conversation started and they were drinking away enjoying themselves. Well, Neva was pouring water over himself not actually drinking it. Trying not to make it blindingly obvious, Francis avoided mentioning Gem to Neva, but failed miserably after only five minutes. Neva understood the ways of humans better than most on the beach. Sure wasn't he an extremely old rock that had witnessed many other things in his own life falling apart? But he possessed a wonderful sense of humour; picked up from mankind so long ago he had forgotten himself.

"Survival!" he shouted, raising his glass and tossing it over himself to the beat of the music.

As two of the witches from the hen party approached the bar, hoping to order more beer and wine, his whole body gave off a misty reaction to the water on his surface, which was scorched under the hot sun.

"Let me get these girls sorted and we will have a chat my friend," he said.

Francis couldn't avoid the first girl's good looks, and equally unable to avoid looking at her breasts, but still looking into her eyes. He smiled. She leaned on the bar, slightly tipsy but friendly. He was daydreaming and knew all his worries would mean nothing. He was a young man in love with a rock; both of them were standing on a larger rock floating through space at the edge of a galaxy full of rocks in the middle of nowhere surrounded by even more bloody rocks way off in the distance of interstellar space. He knew it wasn't love...but wanted the friendship, the closeness. This rejection pissed him off. Staring out to sea, his thoughts were a million miles away. Thinking big again! The cool breeze blowing in from the sea woke him up.

"Wonderful," Francis replied.

Neva gave a curious look from behind the bar.

"What's wonderful?"

Francis looked Neva in the eye; the water slowly evaporating from his face.

"This place is, my friend. This place is wonderful!"

Chapter Fourteen

SANDSTONE

José had spent the last few days invisible as he crept around the beach testing his powerful magic. He listened for hours to conversations about anything and from anyone. But Gem was the thought he returned to every few seconds. Listening to his whispering was EXTREMELY frightening. How he would destroy every living creature on the beach to have her back, to hold her, to control her. The crabs he killed behind the main catapult were a test. He had first made them feel uneasy by moving some small stones around them. Then when both the spider crabs had become so freaked out that they activated their rings, he silently materialised directly before them. They had time to make a defence. But José let flow a trickle of his potential power killing them almost instantly. Passing by on her way home to her mother, the baby sea crab was unfortunately in the wrong place at the wrong time.

José had listened to Alex for ages. He found the conversations of humans very interesting because they were so different than the other creatures on the beach. Humans had such a short life, always rushing about trying to accomplish things that would normally take rocks years, and then some, to attend to. In the beginning he had discovered that Francis and Alex were looking for Sandstone, for whatever reason he still pondered over. But after a few days of listening to her it was plainly obvious she wanted information regarding another human called Jesus. José got bored as he was incapable of seeing past his own lust for Gem. Of all the creatures on the beach only Herman, Smasher and a few powerful individuals even understood the magnitude of Sandstone's true nature.

It had taken Herman almost an hour of gruelling conversation with Smasher to admit that it was better to bring the matter of what was really transpiring to a close as soon as possible. He finally admitted that it was easier to bring Francis and Alex to Sandstone and save all this running about. Both of them knew it was about four o'clock back in Dublin and they should be heading home as their mother would be worried. After what happened to Alex at the kitchen table, being late would make the situation worse. But the temptation was too much to resist. Tonight, they would stay a little longer and that was that.

They had been walking for what seemed an hour, criss-crossing the same route over and over. Herman would say wait a moment and suddenly disappear over some sand dune, to reappear from the other direction a moment later. Francis and Alex were very impressed. Herman was transporting himself to different locations in an attempt to discover if they were being observed. Smasher could feel if something was near, with the assistance of Herman and his rings. All four now stood at the entrance to a small cave that gave the appearance of going deep underneath a massive dune of solid rock covered in sand. The sand was falling to the ground over the entrance making small perfect pyramids below. Herman calmly spoke to Smasher.

"I am doing the right thing Smasher. Letting them see Sandstone. They would have found him anyway even without our help. Let them go and discover what they should."

Francis and Alex carefully entered into this underworld. Inside the air was filled with moisture. Green algae were growing on the rocks near the entrance with small drops of water dripping from the ceiling. Francis was tense with anticipation. His entire brain power was attempting to predict what would be Sandstone's first sentence. Thoughts flashed across his mind: What did Jesus eat? How tall was he? Did he have a beard, a wife, a lover, a sister, a brother? What colour were his eyes? And was he a real human being, actually flesh and blood. Was the whole story true?

Half way into the cave, they spotted a small creature walking about looking at the ground. As they approached, he stopped, picked up something and moved on. He looked very relaxed.

Francis and Alex had spent a few moments staring at him, which was making the meeting a little uneasy - even by a stone's cognition - as Sandstone had not spoken. Alex was still shaking her head from left to right. He had to say something and soon; both of them were on the verge of collapse. After what seemed ages he finally spoke.

"Hi!"

"Hello to you," they both answered.

"What are you up to?" he asked.

"Well, we were looking for you," Alex stuttered.

Not from being afraid but because she knew that whatever was coming was going to change a lot of things for her.

"I, umh, we are overjoyed to meet you Sandstone. May I call you that?"

"Why were you searching for me, and who told you my name?"

"Herman and Smasher. They're above at the entrance to the cave."

At the mention of their names, he recalled fond memories.

"Those two crazy creatures! Yes, I can sense them now. All this time I wondered are they well. Why would you be searching for me down here?"

It took ages for them to get over the fact that they were talking to someone who had met Jesus Christ. Alex started by saying they arrived at the beach some days ago and were travelling between their world and here almost every day. They had made friends with Herman and Smasher and found this place incredible.

"Yes it always has this effect on humans," Sandstone admitted.

As the conversation went on, Francis talked of his world and the famous people who made a great impression on mankind.

"You live such short lives compared to the rest of us here on the beach. But I do remember a few witches and wizards living really long lives," Sandstone paused for a moment. "What was her name? That's lost me for a moment," Sandstone looked up towards the roof of the cave in deep thought.

"No, I can't remember her name. But I do remember much from your world. You are all so crazy! Completely nuts!! I suppose that's what defines you, drives you. If you lived twice as long, you'd chill out. But all things are seen through some other creature's eyes eventually. I have always liked your species. You are remarkable and truly unique to this planet."

He mentioned Alexander of Mesopotamia, the great warrior who tried to rule the world, and Nimrod the builder of The Hanging Gardens of Babylon.

"But long before them, in the age of old that no human knows, was Sil-see. I met him in the lost city of Tillious five thousand years before the pyramids were built.. I am sure you know nothing of what I speak as all was lost in the great fire that destroyed the library at Alexandria."

Francis felt a strange sensation on hearing the name Sil-see. Alex couldn't help noticing like Francis, that Sandstone would twitch as he got to the end of saying that name.

"Sorry Sandstone, but who was Sil-see?" Francis asked.

After saying the word, a shiver ran through his body and the hairs on the back of his neck stood up straight. Sandstone didn't notice the effect the name had on Francis. He was still completely shocked at meeting two young humans.

"Sil-see was a man from what you would call now South Africa. It's another crazy tale, of human endeavour. He walked to Egypt which took him most of his life."

Francis and Alex were dumbfounded. Sandstone hadn't been talking for longer than five minutes but both of them felt like their brains were jumping up and down inside their heads with the excitement of five year old children. It was as if a storm trooper had arrived at their house delivering an invitation to join Darth Vader on the Death Star for a trip round the galaxy giving it hard to the rebels.

Sandstone hadn't talked to a living soul in over a hundred years and seemed to be really enjoying the conversation with Francis and his sister. He knew that there was no danger as he would be the first to notice anything out of the ordinary. With everything so relaxed they continued chatting about absolutely everything. Alex's question regarding the pyramids being landing platforms for alien space ships gave Sandstone a crazy laugh. He chuckled!

"What's so funny?" She asked.

Francis was nearly falling over with laughter listening to her.

"Sadly I have to say no, Alex, they were not meant for landing space ships. When they had left, the Egyptians wanted to build something of such a scale that could be seen from space by them and to emulate the feeling of Gods."

"When *who* left?" Francis curiosity was in overdrive.

"The aliens of course," Sandstone explained.

"You mean *real* aliens?" they both enquired.

"Well yes, and I have no problem telling you both that. In your world, no one will believe you anyway as it was so long ago and there isn't any proof to be found. Actually that's not quite true." He paused for a moment. "There is one piece, from the landings in South America. But I would think it's been long destroyed. It was brought on a ship to Spain and sent to the Vatican. The ship sank in eighty feet of water off the coast at Tarraco in Spain with few survivors. The king went crazy and demanded that the best engineers of the time do something to retrieve the ship as he understood the importance of the cargo. So it was ordered to build a wall out into the sea, past and around the sunken ship and then return the wall to land. Afterwards they removed the water by hand which took a very long time. It was turned into a harbour months later by knocking a hole in the sea wall."

"Eventually, they retrieved the cargo and upon seeing it the king marched an army of five thousand Spanish soldiers across Europe guarding it on the journey to Rome. It's still there below in the vaults of the Vatican. Personally, I never saw it but back then I had so many friends and they said it was a ten foot tall, twenty feet long solid wall of gold with an image of Indians meeting a very strangely dressed bunch of humans and the great story of their journey."

"This is amazing. What you're saying is unreal, Sandstone." Francis sat back onto the cold ground.

"Not really, Francis. What I mean is that I lived through it, that's all. As I said about Sil-see walking the length of Africa. All he did was talk about his life before he died. He had gained a great deal of facts regarding the working of magic, life and the world that also helped me understand much. All his knowledge was from the old world."

"Sorry can we go back to the part about the aliens please? Have they visited us more that once?" Alex asked as calmly as possible given her enthusiasm.

"Not from what I know. They stayed a few years I think, not much longer. They travelled the stars, like you told me you're exploring our beach, nothing more."

"What were they like?" Alex whispered.

"Pale skinned and skinny like you. Maybe they had forgotten what food was," he replied.

Alex was so excited she stopped talking. They were electrified with every word that passed from this five inch tall piece of sandstone. Every time they said a name or mentioned a time in human history he had something to say. As Sandstone was chatting away, Francis was still dreaming of the giant golden wall being transported across Europe by all those soldiers.

"Jesus Christ, it's too much to take in, Alex!"

At the mention of this name Sandstone abruptly stopped talking and stared at both of them.

"You know of him?" Alex asked.

"Did I know Jesus Christ? Of course I knew him. He was a wonderful person and became a great but short lived friend. Those were crazy times," he sighed. "With all the slaughter and butchery going on in that part of the world, he was a welcome sight. I loved listening to him and regret our introduction. I was lying at the side of a road listening to some argument about religion, when a fight started. You humans make such a big deal out of things! Anyway, somebody picked me up and hurled me towards him. I hit him in the head and thus started our brief friendship."

"That's fucking incredible," Francis admitted shocked to the point of collapsing. He still edged forward. "Did he have a wife?"

"Why do you want to know that?" Sandstone was perplexed.

"In our world, a lot of people would like to know that. I understand it's strange. When I was younger I always prayed to God for help. But as I got older so many other things came into my head that I pushed him to the side. It's so good to know he existed, was a real person."

"Francis, Jesus didn't just exist. He was a state of mind. A wakeup call - an injection of clarity into the minds of anyone who wanted to listen. Jesus brought many of you together and tried to remind you what it was to be human. That's all, and no Alex, before you ask, sadly the star of Bethlehem was not a space ship." He nodded with a deep grin of affection towards her.

"Your world is full of variety. Everywhere you look there is something different. It is a simple fact that your species needs some sort of guidance, no matter what your belief. Drawing you to each other in times of need and providing a shield when the lights go out. Of course I understand they also caused wars and lots of trouble. But it is always your humanity that shines through."

"You sound like such a wise old guy." Francis added.

"Well, I learnt a lot from him Francis. I witnessed his death, those who caused it and everything in-between."

Then Sandstone spoke Jesus' name in some strange language and shock his head like the way he did when he mentioned Silsee from Africa. Francis felt a surge of emotion flow though him again. This time Sandstone noticed his reaction. Francis tried to repeat the name and in doing so caused what seemed like a rumbling noise about the cave as dust fell from the ceiling above. With this Sandstone realised Francis and Alex were not all they appeared to be. Searching to the entrance and then returning his glance to both of them, he asked, "Why did Herman and Smasher bring you to see me again?"

Alex could sense that Sandstone's mood and manner were about to change.

"Why didn't I ask you more concerning that?" he asked himself.

Francis was listening but he was distracted because he couldn't stop repeating the word Sandstone had said over and over in his head. He was unaware that he was now lying on his back on the floor of the cave in a deep dream. In his mind he was sinking into the area of sand above on the beach that Gem had called the dead zone. It felt like he was on a boat far out to sea rocking up and down drifting without a course. Waves that were cut open by the vessel's keel all splashed away transformed into sand and he quickly recognised the small mole like creatures that had frightened him were setting the course this ship would sail.

Thousands of heads were bobbing up and down over this ocean of sand and they all seemed different. Francis was still repeating the word inside his head. It relaxed him, comforted him, while all around him the waves got larger and the ship swayed in high seas. Slowly, he discovered that he could control the direction of the ship. Facing it into the large waves while heading for a small island in the distance. It didn't take long before he broke the surf and gracefully landed on a beach of perfect white sand. Upon standing up, he noticed footprints in the sand leading off inland. He sensed somehow it was safe. So he followed blindly. Shaking his head, looking back to the sea, thinking to himself still in a deep dream state, *Why am I doing this?*

At that very moment, a small molehill of sand popped from the ground a few feet ahead of him on the path, its eyes appeared so sorrowful. Francis was still repeating the name Sandstone had told him. The little molehill gestured to follow. Francis did. Why not? he thought. Walking up the beach he glanced down to the molehill beside him. Francis saw a tiny expression in its face. It was grinning.

"Do you understand me?"

There came no verbal response, only a nodding of the head.

"Where are we going?" The creature appeared to shrug its shoulders in an uncertain response.

"Well are you going to show me something?" Francis asked. The creature jumped. A clear expression of yes appeared on its little face.

"Ok now were getting somewhere. Where is it?" he asked cheerfully, delighted that he had overcome the basics of this impossible task. Unfortunately, the creature shrugged again.

"Jesus, what's this shit?" he moaned. "I am sorry, I don't understand."

The creature did nothing except stare back and them slump a little lower into the ground with diminutive puppy eyes. It took Francis a while longer to work out a question that required a simple yes or no from the creature. "Is all this about me?" The creature leaped up and down with excitement.

"Wait a moment; you want me to ask all the questions, don't you?" With this, the creature again leapt from the ground into the air diving back into the sand and repeating the same thing over and over until it seemed out of breath with happiness.

"You want me to talk about my problems at this moment in my life? Oh. Dear God, I can't fucking wait! Do you know I am not having the best of times at the moment?"

The creature tossed two arms into the air and fell backwards into the sand with a huge sigh of relief.

"A friend of mind told me you were all long, lost remains of stones that are somehow trapped and you all cling together to make meaning of the past in some shape or form."

The creature gave no response, and reappeared on the other side of Francis as a smaller molehill, ever so slightly bobbing up and down. They started walking again. Francis found it helped to be moving. Everything seemed to look so good if you were moving past something or it was passing you. It could have been a small village full of cottages when from around the corner comes a huge mining machine of some kind. Towering over the tiny buildings. Francis always found it was more interesting and exciting when something was not quite as it should be. Slightly out of sync he would say.

"I'm out of place, that's why everyone is so interested in me. I'm not where I should be, am I?" The creature nodded in agreement as they walked. "Then where am I meant to be? Sorry, give me a second. I'll rephrase that. Eloïse, I could use you now," he whispered while rubbing his hand over his forehead and dragging it down his face scratching his nose in bewilderment, twice. Rolling his eyes Francis was truly stuck for words.

"Ok! I know I wouldn't be in this mess if I hadn't fallen for a girl, sorry, *stone*. I have been together with other girls, not stones before. You know," Francis gestured towards the molehill. "And, well, it's that we were the best of friends and that's the problem. She destroyed our friendship, and I can't do anything about that. I have no control over anything. You see friendship to me is everything, and I know that sometimes I take a naive look at the world. But that's me. Maybe I was a little too eager also," Francis paused. He was trying to justify his actions. "Does that make any sense to you?"

The creature nodded in agreement with what it had heard.

"Yes?" Francis asked with complete surprise. "Yes to what? I am going insane or I am right? I was used by a spell that made me think we were together for six months not a week, and it hurts. I can see it. And I know she never wanted the same things I wanted. She had all that before and was emotionally destroyed by them herself. And that's why she would never get involved like that again unless she had control."

He looked around, pausing for a moment.

"Damn, damn . . . I hate this shit."

Francis lay down on the soft, white sand. Scooping up large handfuls and then slowly letting them fall to the ground forming tiny hills. Moving his arm slightly to the right he made another and another. By the time he had finished the third one, the first had started moving and two little eyes appeared. Now all three were alive and Francis thought to himself they are being formed as I speak. Here, right now. The original creature that greeted him on the beach in his surreal dream slowly moved around him coming to rest beside the three new life forms.

"Each person we meet, become friends with, talk to on a bus, anywhere, can change you if you're that type of person," He said aloud. Then it dawned on him. *I am still learning, I will always be learning, like it was better to be born naive but mostly it's you don't want to know everything, happy in your little bubble: that's control not stupidity. Others stop and subsequently get stuck in their lives, like a bad job.*

"Your way Francis, that's all, because I discover as I go along," he decided.

Streaming flashes of light resembling comets jetted across the sky above him. Clearly visible was the difference in speed. Some ticking along over the sky like old faithful in Yellow Stone National Park, while others drifted around with what appeared like no control. Yet others would speed up for a moment, as if requiring all their energy to catch up. Only to fall behind again and repeat the action when they had enough energy saved. There were millions, no, billions, as out further in the sky were countless masses of comets roaring through the blackness of space. Francis understood the uniqueness of their journey.

With an expression resembling relief he bid farewell to the creature and its three new very happy friends as he started walking back towards the sea surrounding this tiny island. Reaching the ocean of sand, he slid into it with all the grace and magnitude of a White Star line ship being launched into the great ocean.

Chapter Fifteen

NEW POWER

Sandstone and Alex were beside Francis as he opened his eyes.

"Look! He's awake!" Alex shouted.

"So he is. Considering what has happened, that's surprising. How do you feel?" Sandstone asked with concern.

Francis had no idea that he had survived an incredible ordeal of mental control. Not that Francis could have been killed but if he hadn't worked out what was happening and used his imagination to reach a point of understanding he would not have awoken and the little island would have become his home for a very long time. Awkwardly, with the assistance of Alex Francis got to his feet. He was now staring down at Sandstone.

"What happened was amazing," he said.

"No. It's frighteningly amazing. You overcame the trap! That's impossible I would have thought for a human. It's too complex. You couldn't have done that without assistance," Sandstone was getting angry. "How did you do that? HOW?" he shouted.

His eyes were rolling, looking in all directions searching every corner of the cave for an answer. "You worked it out didn't you? What's with you? Who *are* you?"

Directly following his last word, he dropped the handful of little pebbles he was holding. One by one, they started trickling from his grip, hitting the cave floor each smashing into the ground. The moment of silence that followed caused an unexpected amount of tension within the cave. One would have felt attached to the walls, like living, breathing every single grain of sand, rock, every microbe, as though the very dampness itself gliding through the air; that it could only be understood by the expressions on the faces of both Francis and Sandstone as they became aware of the magnitude of that which Francis was now part. Alex was starting to look concerned because Sandstone took a worrying few steps in the direction of Francis, all the time holding his stare up to him.

"Why do you want to hurt my brother?" she said with all the force of a young woman. Quickly, she held onto Francis arm.

Sandstone sent a mental message to Herman and Smasher above at the entrance. They came running into the cave. Smasher kept bashing his head on the ceiling causing a trail of dust behind them both. Herman was the first to speak.

"It's good to see you old friend, what happened?"

"He understands another name I had for a human friend a long time ago. I don't know how but he survived the test. Herman he understands the meaning of the name!"

"How's that even possible?" he answered shocked.

Meanwhile, Francis was trying not to think of the word but it popped into his head again. The air in the cave was moving towards Francis. As he was dreaming, it was actually happening around him. Exactly then, the cave appeared empty of life because everyone was so still and quiet. Francis Williams suddenly gave it more life. At that very moment, Sandstone started chanting a spell and Herman was rattling his rings in readiness to defend against whatever was about to happen, because they had no idea what was coming next. However, it became obvious as soon as they felt the ground beneath them move! All around everyone's feet, lush green grass slowly emerged upwards.

Herman looked to Sandstone and they both knew all was ok. Right there and then they all sat down. The truth was told regarding everything for the benefit of Sandstone. He didn't ask he demanded to know everything of the two young humans while Herman and Smasher vouched for them both. Herman was nervous about the events of the last few days especially since some innocent creatures had already been killed. Sandstone was furious to learn that José had returned from the deep and was hell-bent on causing mayhem. He had made it very clear to all that he wished for nothing better than to hear of his demise. Francis now possessed this new power of which he had no understanding, and this made matters worse.

Alex explained that their friend the witch had given them the candle. Sandstone and Herman needed to be sure that Eloïse was playing on their side. Sandstone was searching his mind, reaching for the memory. Herman beat him to it by a second.

"Over a hundred and fifty years ago was the last time I saw her. She was no-one special. If she even is that person. Alex what does this Eloïse do in your world?" Herman asked.

"She is a shopkeeper."

After nearly an hour of discussion in the cave, Herman and Sandstone were convinced that Francis understood how powerful the name of Jesus was when spoken in this other language and worse still because he had such a strong imagination and would appear to be in the middle of a lost-lust-love situation regarding a girl he had helped to create. Multiplying their worries regarding him. Francis had agreed not to say the word aloud, even to Alex.

Deep down Francis was someone who had no wish to change, but understood all things evolve at some level. He would have the same nature all his life, and was now in the right place at the right time. He looked to the others thinking the same. How could this all have transpired by accident when Simon Peg as a Met Officer convinced the world by saying, a collision implied someone was at fault?

Sandstone wished everyone well as they all left. He refused to accompany them back to the beach, but asked Herman to keep him informed of all events. Alex reminded Francis with a little urgency that they needed to return home now. Smasher placed one of his large fingers on the shoulder of Alex in an expression of friendship.

"Return safely and see you both soon my friends."

Francis used the moment to thank them deeply for all he had done this day. It was clear to see the lifted spirits in Francis. The little crab was delighted that he was moving forward. Lost in thought, they both started walking to the top of a nearby sand dune. Alex saw her brain slowly sinking into what appeared to be a swamp surrounded by all the events of the past day. Yawning, she didn't even bother holding her hand to cover her mouth as it wasn't necessary. They both looked exhausted. Quickly, they unpacked the candle and lit it. A few moments later they had returned to Francis' bedroom.

Francis went straight to the bathroom to toss water on his face and clean his teeth in an attempt to try and hide the smell of alcohol from his breath. Two moments later, all his clothes were on the floor as he decided a shower was best.

Alex crept down the staircase to the front door. Looking about like a criminal, she approached like a ninja. Opened it quietly, and then slammed it shut from the inside.

"Mum, we're back!" she shouted.

Her mother ran from the kitchen at the back of the house still holding a dinner plate in her hand as she had been busy setting the table.

"Where have you been I called you ten times?" she asked.

"Sorry Mum. I turned it off and forgot."

"How are you feeling, and where's your brother?" She kissed her daughter on the cheek.

"I feel much better Mum and very hungry. Francis is upstairs having a wash he got covered in sand down on the beach."

Alex's mother walked her hand on shoulder through the house to the kitchen for a nice cup of tea.

The next two hours passed off normally as their mother was more interested in Alex's health. After dinner, Francis went upstairs and watched TV in his room. It was around nine o'clock when he said good night to his parents and went to bed. They would not be returning to the beach tonight. Both of them needed a break and a good night's sleep.

Francis flung his clothes to the ground and slipped under the covers. He was instantly asleep and dreaming to the tune of the music still playing on TV. How could he contain all that he had seen the last day? Even thinking about trying to explain to another person was too much. But he knew what had happened, having witnessed it all with his own eyes. As he fell into a deep sleep all that showed on his face was a broad smile.

"Francis! Francis!" His mother repeated as she shook his body in the bed a number of times. His response was slow and grumpy.

"Let me sleep," he pleaded in a hushed voice pulling the covers back over his head.

"It's nearly eleven o'clock. Come on, GET OUT OF BED!" She shouted, pulling the covers completely off the bed.

"I'M ON SUMMER BREAK!" he screamed back.

"Don't you shout at me like that young man! Now get up. I've been to mass and back already."

Francis was totally exhausted and started ranting.

"Lucky you. How was Jesus, good? Did he look ok, or did his friends drop by in their space ship to say hello?"

"I am warning you Francis not to make fun of my beliefs," she snapped.

"Mum, I was wondering was there any news on his return?"

For the last six years, Francis' mother had this argument with her son knowing it was his way to rebel. So she left him to think over his choice of words. Better to say nothing sometimes she thought. Next, she walked into Alex's room to find her daughter lying on the bed, eyes open looking at the roof.

"Morning Alex, all good my dear?" She sat down beside her on the bed.

"Jesus had a wife and kids, Mum."

As her expression turned to shock, their mother breathed in an enormous intake of air.

"Dear God! What has Francis been telling you?"

Chapter Sixteen

GOLDEN SHOWER

All the creatures on the beach were resting from an exhausting day of the games. Stones don't get tired like humans but they do need to slow down, unwind, and enjoy the silence. Most were lying around awake; many had their eyes closed. Many were still deep in conversations regarding the more memorable moments from the opening day of the games. They had enjoyed the darkness of last night. Now small waves broke with ease onto the shoreline.

Far out to sea on the horizon, an orange glow was slowly making its way into the sky. It was magnificent to say the least. The stones were shaking, all the crystals gems sparkled. It was a carpet of living creatures reacting to the early morning sun.

The warm light reminded them of the beautiful day arriving while they appeared to be turning in their beds for a more comfortable position. The clattering could be heard a mile away. It was around this time every morning when hundreds of thousands of crabs emerged from the sea. Every shape, size and colour imaginable came ashore moving slowly towards the stones. It resembled an image of a shift ending in a huge factory far away in China: thousands of bodies going in every direction. The blockage caused by a red light at a pedestrian crossing held back hundreds, but they still kept streaming out from inside the factory.

Something was very different on this morning, though. The first crabs on the beach looked uneasy and were scampering at full speed now onto the first stones about fifty feet onshore. Looking back at their brethren, pouring forth from the ocean; an unusually large amount even for the games. A considerable number of the stones already knew what was up. An invisible force was pushing the crabs forward. By this time, all the noise had roused half the beach. Every crab on shore was now looking out to sea. They were not afraid but excited. A distance out, the water was lifting slowly in parts as if something wanted to break free from the surface of the ocean itself.

To the left of this, another strange movement of water appeared off-shore. This phenomenon was like nothing many creatures had ever observed on the beach. Everyone appeared confused, the majority staring in one direction with awe. To some, it was whales coming up for air, as its back pushes out of the water to breathe. The crabs now knew what it was and waited for the first to surface. In all, there were eight of these mounds pushing the water forward, heading for the beach. Then this creature about fifty feet across started rising from the sea. A small island full of water flowed from its centre to fall by its side. The crabs on the beach went crazy. Thousands snapping their claws together jumping into the air, as a giant sea crab came marching from the deep. With the sun behind, it resembled a walking oil rig towering into the heavens. Instantly, the entire beach was aware of what was happening and experienced euphoria. The word spread as fast as lightning. Within seconds, everyone knew that a very special event was about to occur.

Herman appeared frozen as he also understood. He was resting on a stone chair in Smasher's house. Instinctively, he leaped for Smasher's hand and he took half the wall from the side of his door, ramming into a group of stones who were completely out of control charging in the direction of the beach. Such an event was this that there was no time for apologies. Every single stone that wasn't on the beach was racing to it. These monsters of the deep moved as leviathans with millions of litres of water flowing from their bodies. As the first walked onto the shore, thousands of stones lined up for the greatest shower in history.

It was long told that the great creatures return from the sea every once and a while to cleanse the bitterness and hurt from the inhabitants of the beach. If you could stand under one as he walked passed, and were lucky enough to catch the water flowing off their back, you would be blessed and cleaned. There were already arguments going on under the first. It appeared to be fighting not a blessing. Even the master of ceremonies from the games could be seen pushing and shoving for a better position.

The quiet became loud, the shy became boisterous. Cheering from the crowd was starting to turn non-believers into church-goers because the proof was walking towards them. The second giant crab walked onto the shore. It stopped abruptly and a million litres of sea water came crashing down from above. That was the final trigger. Crabs were lashing out at stones and vice-a-verse. Everyone wanted a piece of the action. Fifty meters down the beach three of the giants came together. An entire section of the beach was racing, scurrying towards them. It was locusts after a field of corn. Larger stones showed total disregard for those beneath as they pushed their way to the forefront of the charge. Within a few minutes, the inhabitants of the beach appeared different to the eye. Everyone looked better, cleaner. In moments, grime of hundreds, even thousands of years were washed away. Every crab was shining in the sunlight and everyone knew it. Which drove them all crazy as the effects were happening so quickly.

Smasher had carried Herman the mile from his house to the very centre of the crowd, which now resembled a full scale riot. Although they were fighting, somehow it was still fun! Herman was shaking his legs so the rings would fall to the lower part of his feet. While about him creatures battled it out for a better position, directly over- head was Smasher holding ground as this massive crab's leg moved above him. The giant crabs were covered in sea anemones. The reaction with air caused them to release a chemical which turned the water into a "golden shower" as the crabs called it. Smasher stood firm. His entire body was covered with hundreds of smaller stones beneath screaming in ecstasy. And every crab within ten feet was climbing his legs, catching all the water they could. It flowed into his mouth and he gurgled loudly swinging his head back. Spitting it out, the water landed on a family of basalt stones whose appearance was as if they were stage diving to the Prodigy.

And down the water kept coming. Herman looked to be on fire; steam rising from his body as though he had spent a day inside a sauna. He was shivering to help the water reach every section of his body. It was truly fantastic, with another three giant crabs to come.

Even with the great strength of the stones and the rings of the crabs, creatures were getting seriously hurt. New cracks appeared in stones. Heads bashed in the mill vying for the best position. Younger crabs could be seen limping away with life-threatening injuries. Hopefully, this could be fixed later with magic.

Finally, the last two massive creatures emerged from the water delivering the end to a gift not seen in a thousand years.

One was met with a wave of bodies, literally throwing themselves against its legs. The crab had no wish to hurt anyone and it appeared to be doing its best to avoid stepping on someone. But the determination of the remaining creatures to be cleansed, after seeing the results of the others, spurred everyone on.

Eventually the last remaining crab made its way across the beach to the higher dunes two miles inland. Even though only a trickle of water was flowing from their bodies a few stragglers were beneath them following for every drop. Most of the beach was lying on their backs smiling in their newfound beauty. It was an incredible sight. Everyone looked new. Gone were all the stains of age, barnacles fell to the ground in their thousands. A dense mist descended on the beach. What remained was shining, lustful youth.

Herman and Smasher were busy inspecting themselves from head to toe, and surrounded by others doing exactly the same. If you were a few miles away it would look like a giant digital image of our spiral galaxy, the Milky Way from a side view head on. The centre was a mass of light slowly dissipating out to its edges. Many of these beautiful lights shined as our sun does, others as great supernovas. But moving through this galaxy was a beautiful shimmering comet. Its brightness out shone every living creature as she walked from the centre towards the outer edge. Nobody could resist. And for what lasted ages it drifted in the cosmos, among the stars until she came to rest beside Herman and Smasher. Old friends kissed and hugged. Squinting was Smasher's only option as Gem had definitely had a wash.

"Well it's about time you lot had a shower!"

They giggled as children do. Overjoyed with what could be described as rebirth, a large crowd assembled at The Cock Tavern. Pounding music convinced everyone the option was to party. For hours the celebration continued and the terrible event of the killing of the crabs and the return of José faded for a while from the memories of many creatures. Herman trotted about Smashers feet trying to show him how clean he looked from every angle. It was a short distraction. They were both fully aware now would be the perfect time for him to attack.

Gem was at this exact moment surrounded by hundreds of creatures in a massive group inspecting each other's new, clean appearance. José, of course, simply didn't care about anything except getting Gem back. He never even comprehended loosing. His time was spent in fantasyland, wallowing in complete madness, planning what his next move would be. Gem was sitting on the sand, talking to some friends. It started with a few wandering thoughts at the back of her mind; *a passing breeze on a summer night*. Moments later, the thoughts had already disappeared, only to return a few seconds later.

Gem was totally unaware these images were being projected into her mind from José ten feet away. They started slowly enough. She had feelings of warmth, clear skies and long, dry days making her relaxed. *No worries, no stress,* was the impression she was giving off to the world. Then this delightful daydream ended with a vision of how she originally ended up in a nightmare. She started to laugh which was part of his plan, and it would have worked if their relationship had not been so crazy. Without warning, the nightmare returned to her and so did José.

Beside Gem, a number of stones were distracted by movement in the sand that from first appearance resembled a creature walking strangely; but the creature wasn't fully visible. It was a hazy shape. A number of crabs also noticed this but it was by then impossible to escape as they themselves were frozen solid. With the laughter abruptly changing to fear, everyone in the surrounding area also understood they couldn't move. Smasher looked to Herman with shock as they both knew what was happening but were too late. Every creature within a short distance of Gem, including her, were frozen. Terror registered in all of their eyes. Gem's heart, if she had one, started pounding for the wrong reasons. Right at her feet, José appeared slowly from his invisible protective spell. As chameleon changes colour the surrounding beach took his form, as he crawled towards her.

She was terrified. Her mind racing to fight against the power he had.

Smasher was using his entire strength attempting to move but to no avail. He stopped after two attempts, unable to break free. His fists clenched so tight that dust fell to the ground.

Herman knew this spectacle was for show. Why not kill all of us he thought?

José had reached Gem's toes frozen in the sand. He walked onto her foot and started up her leg. The sight was disturbing. He paused to smell her leg for a moment. Continuing upwards he crept like a sickening rash past her knee. Gem fell unconscious, unable to find the power to beat this entrapment; she sought safety within her mind. Her body was changing shape, returning to the form of a stone, melting in front of everyone powerless to help. Every single creature trapped within the area of José spell would have leapt to their feet and started running for their lives if they could have.

Then, as if from nowhere, Eric arrived with solider crabs, that were outside the frozen area of the spell. Many lunged at José with their pincers that could cut cold steel. They were repelled by some invisible force field protecting him. Dazed and confused it took a moment for them to stand again. Sadly many were not moving but lying on their backs motionless. Eric was travelling at great speed in a circle around José. Using the power of his rings he fired energy blasts which bounced off as sparks from this protective barrier surrounding José.

Herman struggled with an incantation. He was unable to move his legs and use the full power of his rings. After what felt an eternity, he was free. From his left claw he shot a bolt of deadly light towards José. Smashing through the protective barrier it struck him head on. He slid backwards visibly feeling the powerful energy pushing him. The protective barrier was what saved his life. But again he appeared unharmed. With combined madness and rage showing on his face, he sent another blast back at Herman. Released from the first spell, Herman was prepared and deflected the bolt of lethal energy. The light flickered across the faces that witnessed this out-of-control bonfire. With the spell broken, anyone who could stand moved back fast. Smasher's fist was already a good ten feet above where José was standing and it impacted the sand a second later.

When the dust had settled, a cold voice devoid of feeling whispered on the breeze. "I will have what is mine; stand in my way and you will die."

Thankfully, only a small part of the beach was witness to this, which was better for everyone concerned. José was out for revenge, he was trying to destroy the fabric of the beach itself.

Moments later, she returned to the form of a girl. She was helped to her feet and led away from the scene with a few other injured creatures. Hundreds of crabs had formed a wide circle around the area of the battle. In the centre lay six dead and fifty shaken solider crabs.

"NOW you understand the power this little bastard has, I hope," Herman roared.

Eric and his men removed the bodies and brought the injured to the far end of the beach.

"We will use magic to assist."

Within three minutes, the area was clear. Anyone passing by would have wondered what had happened as there was a crowd looking on at absolutely nothing for all was now removed.

Up the beach Gem was in a terrible state. Her mind was ranting rubbish as her hideous memories of the imprisonment with José had flooded back.

"No way will I return to that again", she repeated again and again, Screaming as friends tried to comfort her, she ranted, "He destroyed my life. I gave him everything and he used me, used, used, and used me for everything until the very end. I said it then never again will a creature control me."

Gem was of course stating why she didn't want a relationship with Francis. But really, were stones that acted as girls meant to be dating humans? She didn't stop and think about that but she subconsciously understood herself. Her life was consumed by it. From the very first relationship she had done the same thing. There was nothing strange about it. To be honest, it was a human attribute. People are like that. Letting an individual inside your life, getting involved, revealing your feelings, to find out later they are using, controlling, manipulating your life to their own ends and needs.

Chapter Seventeen

ATTACK

Sitting in his room waiting to return to the beach, for Francis the pain of being dumped was akin to the lingering smell of dampness on your clothes. He couldn't remove it. He was talking to himself about the subject, Gem that is, as it was the only way he could find to help himself. As his mind drifted around her image his thoughts returned to the power given to him, by accident, from Sandstone. How incredibly extraordinary his life had become. What a great gift he had been given. One he barely understood and yet he felt safe with because his mind was constantly distracted with thoughts of Gem.

He had many friends who had left at least fifty unread text messages on his phone. This was strange, very peculiar him not answering friends. The summer holidays were flying past and his mother was passing on information regarding which one had called to the house hoping to catch him home. His mother kept informing them he was down on the local beach with his sister. But of course the beach they visited every day had a very different affect on people. Another obsession he thought, another obsession fading over time. Sadly that wasn't the only thought popping in and out from his head. Revenge was present and very pushy. It had a face; someone hassling you for money on the street. One could see it, feel it, punch it because of a reason, even a purpose. But the guilt had a price which most normal people can't handle, unless one can justify the reason or purpose.

Francis pushed his long fingers up through his hair. Every time he closed his eyes her face appeared, and the circle was reformed once more with the river of madness having breached the dam walls to splash down into the village and kill the entire population. As he was sniggering at the thought of the buildings crashing down, Alex came walking into the room. Happily, she sat down on the end of the bed. Francis couldn't help himself and immediately starting talking about Gem and the trouble of the last few days. It was painkillers working as soon as you swallow the tablets. Less pain if you talk about it. Alex understood well enough as she had many guys chasing her for a date, and knew too well Francis had been having it rough.

"What should I do?" Alex asked.

"Be normal to her because we're still going to be friends . . . maybe," he replied. Now Francis made a little jump of fate there, because he was still in love, or in lusting, with Gem.

"What time is it?" He took a deep breath.

"Ten," Alex said.

"So let's get a good night's sleep and head around 11:00 tomorrow morning."

"Fine. Sleep well, Francis." She left his room.

At precisely 11.00am Dublin time the following morning, Francis and Alex materialised in the same spot as always in the centre of a street round the corner from Smasher's house. It was nothing grand, a small flash of light.

For whatever reason the creatures of the beach hadn't taken on the task of naming streets. Most lived in the open under the stars and loved the changing weather beside the ocean. "Fucking Fantastic" was what Francis wanted to name the street but it was way down on the list of things to do. All he wanted was to see Gem as he dropped his head. *What the hell am I doing?* he thought. *Why do I feel I have to stay away from my new friends? because she is on the same beach I don't have to leave.*

"Fuck that!" he said out loud.

They both started walking the hundred metres to the street corner where Alex and himself first heard Herman and Smasher fighting. Francis had never been in this position with a girl before, he hated it. Constantly thinking of Gem; his eyes were feeding his brain a multitude of images. No matter how unimportant, they were being processed: a bird on a wall, water dripping from a broken pipe, strange looking plants growing on a rooftop, or his younger sister as she walked along. Then Gem popped back into his head. He knew he was obsessed, but that's normal after the way he was treated; as he felt connected to her. But sadly he was doing nothing to help let her go.

Although staying friends with her is what he wanted, an explanation was much more important. Holding this thought, his mind sailed across a void of darkness, left far behind our sun and planet earth; its light would provide sight for eons, sadly not for the full distance and meaning of his voyage. He would journey to the end of the universe for her. Alarm bells of reason were sounding in his head. *Only if she didn't behave as a bitch*, he thought.

"Funny but we haven't seen a single creature since we arrived," Alex said.

"They're probably down on the beach watching the games."

They both looked about. It was peculiar; absolutely no-one was around. Not even a pebble?

It took a few moments to reach the three small cottages at the end of the road. Francis was thinking about them for the last hundred metres as one belonged to Gem and so perhaps he might bump into her. Or she might be sitting out front. Or she may be nearby. The amounts of variations on the possibility of meeting were too much. He stopped because it sounded ridiculous, not because it wasn't a possibility. As they passed, Alex did notice a sudden change in Francis. It was as if for a moment he was acting in a play, right before you go on stage. The last minute adjustments to appearance, made him appear different. He was someone else, not himself. Quickly she recognised he couldn't act.

They jumped up the small dune leading to the dead zone. Crossing was easy for the most part as they were unafraid, but as the creatures started appearing behind them they increased their speed to avoid any contact. Continuing to the top of the rise, they were both shocked at the sight that awaited them.

Everyone was shining. Walking forwards both Francis and Alex faces were gleaming with delight as they started to see such beautiful colours in all of the creatures. Two small crabs ran past them their colours bright orange and red. All about the beach creatures looked positively radiant.

Beautiful, they looked beautiful!

"Francis look," Alex pointed to a stone they previously considered to be a loner or simply stuck-up after his bad manners towards her the previous day.

"Whatever did this got him talking, changed his mood."

The creature was surrounded by a large crowd that appeared to be enjoying his jokes. Francis wanted to find Herman and Smasher but it was very hard to see anybody at a distance. Francis reached for his bag and grabbed his shades. Alex also had a pair that were less trendy but worked. They decided to head straight for Neva's bar.

When they arrived there, the party was rocking with hundreds of creatures in attendance. Many were dancing to the music and Smasher was standing in the middle above everyone else, which helped immensely in finding him. They had to push their way through. Smaller crabs were hanging on to the heads and shoulders of other creatures dancing to Daft Punk.

All the stones were washed clean, their different chemical composition could be seen properly, so it appeared that they had skin. Coloured light reflected from the crabs like a disco. It was an incredible display. The heat from the sun was belting down onto their bodies. The crabs giving off the effect of a laser light show. Yellow, orange, bright red sparkled over the dance floor. Looking for a drink, Francis and Alex danced their way to the middle of the crowd. Neva greeted them with a smile as he approached. Before Francis could move his lips Neva had opened a bottle of cold beer and handed it to him. Drinking fast as it was so refreshing; it took a few moments for Francis to get his bearings.

"What the hell happened?" he shouted over the music.

"I know, it's amazing, isn't it? We got a Golden Shower after sunrise. I never dreamed it would happen during my time on the beach."

"Everyone looks so young and happy. Not to mention clean," Francis said.

Neva looked questioningly at Francis for a moment.

"Now I didn't mean anything by that Neva. The crabs look beautiful and the colours in the stones look incredible. Please say you understand me, mate."

Neva let Francis squirm a little longer seeing the embarrassment on his face.

"Yeah we needed a wash, thanks!" he said giving him a bear hug.

"It's been a thousand years I'm told, man we must have stunk."

"Well, yes, you did actually. You stank of earth and sea, and now there's nothing," Francis explained.

"We've been reborn, Francis. Think if a new rock arrives tomorrow. They would be considered a social outcast."

With this they both laughed loudly. Neva then proceeded to toss a glass of water over himself revealing for a short moment even more beautiful elements that made him the rock he was. Francis started to notice so many different minerals that had been impossible to see before. Presently they showed as clear as day the unique combination of his wonderful character. Neva was a mix of, well, so many types of rock from every layer of the earth. Neva put his arm over Francis' shoulder and walked him towards a table with two empty seats. It had the appearance of a chill-out room in some fashionable night club. Beautiful crystal women were being drooled over by stones that suddenly matched their personalities.

Without the protection of the shades he was wearing Francis would have found it difficult to see. Neva started to explain what had happened with the giant sea crabs. Peering out from under his shades to see the real world Francis was astounded by how amazing they all looked. He then informed Francis about the attack from José.

"Crabs were killed others very seriously injured."

Francis immediately was on edge after hearing this news. Waiting impatiently. He couldn't stand it so started interrupting Neva.

"Gem?"

"She was the focus of the attack, Francis, and it was terrifying. Herman, Smasher and about another five hundred creatures were powerless until Herman broke free from the magic and stopped José's rampage. She is shaken up as José re-woke in her mind the full memories of the time spent with that evil little bastard."

Francis sat back onto a stool of solid stone and took a long drink from the bottle of cold beer. Refreshed, he looked around the table. He didn't notice but his breathing had increased slightly. Thoughts flashed across his eyes. Again, he drank.

"Neva, would you mind getting me another beer please?" He was completely calm.

"Sure."

Alone he sat across from an orange fire crystal like the one they were introduced to at the beginning of this week. He studied the tiny stars spurting from her mouth as they drifted into the air above her head. There they grew into shapes, not so unlike the creatures of the beach. When they formed into an identifiable shape the wind would simply deform it as with the trails left by aeroplanes high in the sky.

News of the attack angered Francis immensely, although he remained calm. He was now forced to concentrate harder on the matter at hand: the tortuous death of José. Neva returned a short time later with refreshments and Francis' vision came to an abrupt end, thankfully. He worried for Gem and tried to control his emotions when talking to Neva. This crazy mix of stone knew too well Francis was feeling the after-affects of being dumped as he had seen it before.

It was exactly the same with José all those years ago. Exactly. Neva had no intention of telling Francis that most of the creatures on the beach knew José well. Many would have considered him a brother before this trouble began. Choosing to leave that story for Herman who, at some point, would have to inform him. Instead he told him Gem was recovering at Smasher's house, shaken by the attack but doing fine.

This news didn't help Francis. He wanted to see her, offer assistance as a friend. Worse still he was feeling a crazy jealousy that his new friends were there and he wasn't. That was killing him because he lost a friend. No matter if she had dumped him. He felt a connection with her as that's what mattered to him. If he asked how she was doing would his friends think he was hoping to see her? He shook his head and cleared his thoughts of the paranoia, and started chatting to Neva about the giant sea crabs.

The dancing crowd had grown larger and larger surrounding The Cock Tavern. Its surge was pressing hard against the creatures sitting down. The music was now pounding, thumping dance. Alex was having a hard time reaching the seating area but managed by standing on top of a few dancing rocks and jumping down onto the soft sand close to Neva and Francis. Alex gave him a kiss on his cheek, which he returned with a loving low five. As soon as she sat down, he forced Neva to repeat the story of the giant crabs. He was happy to oblige and Francis was eager to forget about Gem.

Some fifty solider crabs and various other creatures surrounded Herman as he tried to magically fix a broken head. The majority of the injured had been treated for their wounds with the help of magical means: busted legs being bent back into shape, bleeding heads electrically sealed as a welder would melt two metal plates together in a shipyard. It was an amazing sight. Blinding white light, similar to watching magnesium strip burning in chemistry class at school.

Ten crabs had been killed, one hundred other creatures injured during the brief battle. It was a terrible sight. The bodies were taken to the water's edge and wrapped in seaweed for their return to the ocean. As the law with crabs stood, they must reach the sea before the day's end or drift in the human world forever. Gem had been filling buckets with sea water from a small outcrop of rock beside the sea, and then carried by volunteers to allow the wounded crabs to rest and, of course, heal faster in their own environment. She was very disturbed by the attack but needed to do something, feel busy and forget.

Herman's relief was obvious as another life was saved. This little crab two inches across had a cracked skull and was not moving. He was leaning to the left lying on his claws. Herman was welding his head together. Controlling a micro fine beam of light coming from his claws. The youngster awoke startled. At that moment cold seawater was poured over his body. Shaking himself, he arose to the delight of all.

After this Herman looked up to everyone around him in that far corner of the beach, and openly said. "We can't beat José alone. I know that. His magic, it's different somehow. It felt strange nothing I know. He was never that powerful."

They discussed this for ages adding little bits of information now and again regarding the spells, incantations and the means to cast them. Herman understood they would have to get a lot more help. Everyone wanted to kill José no matter what the cost.

"We will need the help of Francis, the human, *and* Gem. Their assistance will be our edge to cast José into the deep forever. We have a full day of games to play. He will not stop them."

Chapter Eighteen

MIXED FEELINGS

Heading back along the beach they both saw the images of the dead crabs fresh in their minds. Gem was holding Herman as they walked. Passing a friend, he gave the odd claw up in greeting. Nothing would stop the enjoyment of the games for the thousands of creatures on the beach. But, in the background was the enemy, a very nasty enemy. Nearing the party at The Cock Tavern their moods lifted by hearing the music. More friends greeted them and, for a while, everything was normal.

Seeing Gem arrive, Francis was very uncomfortable, he couldn't be himself. He was sure she felt the same. Their eyes met and both looked away. They glanced at each other again when the other was turned away and they both knew this. Francis couldn't stand it any longer so moved away to talk with Herman. He informed him what had happened the last day and it over-shadowed the great event of the giant crabs coming ashore to cleanse the beach's inhabitants.

Francis had another beer and kind of forgot about Gem for a while. He was dreaming he was flying as a sea bird gliding on the wind searching for lunch. He had no idea where he was getting the energy from, but it didn't matter. He didn't need wings to fly, but he saw himself as having two. He used the wind to soar higher and higher into the sky, forgetting the trouble with Gem and José. He was feeling free and it showed. Neva was playing some funky tunes and everyone was dancing and screaming with joy at being there. In his mind, Francis flew on the wind for ages. Over great seas and landmasses he travelled, exploring everything he ever wanted.

It was about 1:00p.m. many of the party goers were slowly breaking off and heading to the stands for the day's games. Francis had managed to build up enough courage to talk to Gem, for the sake of his own sanity; he wasn't looking to get back together or annoy her. He wanted one chance for her to explain her actions and how she felt. This was, of course, only normal after what had happened yesterday. Unfortunately for Francis she lost the plot in front of everyone. It was plainly obvious that she was pissed off with the fact that he was even around. Francis had many new friends on the beach, though. What was he meant to do? Never come back to see Herman and Smasher again?

Like a ship slowly drifting away from its moorings when it shouldn't be, he approached Gem feeling very detached. He couldn't hide it and though he tried desperately to do so this made it look even worse.

"Gem, I need to talk to you. It's that I need to clear the rubbish from my head," he said, like a slave looking for the day off. He was of course being polite.

"Listen, Francis, we are finished, OK! I don't have any feelings for you anymore so stop fucking annoying me. Leave me alone, it's over," she shouted.

Francis didn't even have the chance to think. He had not expected the conversation to happen in this manner with so many others listening in.

"You cause me any hassle and I will make your life very difficult," she said with complete conviction.

"I wanted to tell you something," he stuttered.

But she had already left. Francis stood there like a man frozen.

Herman was sitting nearby on top of a pillar. Lowering his head with a very saddened expression, he slowly made his way down to the ground. Then he leapt from one creature's leg to another to cross this path full of life heading for the games. His jumps were relaxed and controlled to reach Francis. Climbing up his leg he started talking and this should have helped Francis. But it was too late as he was already dreaming with his new power. Everything surrounding him started to bend and twist, even the air.

Herman felt the effect as did every other creature about. They were not feeling pain or distress. Back and forth they bent like plastic, being warped out of shape. It was as if being the water itself inside a giant fish bowl as a Supreme Being pushed it back and forth. With every movement, water went thundering up one side to come crashing down onto the other.

"Francis stop! What are you doing?" Herman asked with worry.

"Oh, letting someone know I am on the beach."

With that comment Francis was indeed standing in the centre of this giant fish bowl underwater. It appeared everyone was swirling around out of control. Then, without warning, the beautiful wave departed from Francis in every direction outward. Growing like the ripple effect from dropping a large stone into a pond as it spread forward connecting every living creature on the beach. For a millisecond it touched them and turned them into a substance that acted like water as this invisible wave went past. When it reached Gem, her world paused as if she was frozen in time. Her shoulders pulled backwards and her chest pushed forward slowly as when you stretch after you wake to a sunny day. Bending into all sorts of directions, her brain felt fuzzy.

Herman could say nothing but be impressed. He was clinging to Francis' t-shirt.

"You see, I didn't hurt anyone, Herman. I wanted to stretch my fingers."

"Walk, Francis. You don't want to bring any more attention to yourself than necessary. But I'd say after that little trick even the damn insects will know you're responsible."

Remarkable as it may seem, not a handful of creatures would have guessed Francis, the human, had possessed enough power to beset every living creature on the beach at once with such a soft feeling of happiness. They had assumed Francis had started walking first. The fact that Herman was on his shoulder gave him much respect from the rocks and any question of his involvement was immediately thrown aside. But the problem was that everyone loved the invisible wave of enjoyment. There was the odd cheer of "More! More!" as the crowed continued in the direction of the games. Names for the mad wave had already spread the entire length of the beach and back again. "The Happy Mexican" was one "Oh Yeah" was another. The list of fresh, positive feelings was endless. Which of course added to the whispers of whom, or what was responsible for that joyous feeling and why?

Francis however was feeling less than happy. On the outside everything was presented as a perfect story, but dark clouds on the horizon was a better description for his state of mind. In fact, he was about to crack which was probably not the best outcome for anyone in his position but something had to give. The spell that Gem had held over him was completely broken. It was extremely difficult for him to concentrate. It felt like he had been consuming drugs for six months and was experiencing very painful withdrawal symptoms. He had broken up with her the previous day and already his world had imploded because of her magic and what he had also given her: his feelings. His friends saw Gem more than himself, pushing his paranoia to new extremes.

Ok they were friends longer that he could even imagine. But Herman and Smasher would be those friends you make in your thirties. The ones you don't have to grow up with and somehow are as strong, or stronger, relationships. It wasn't that he was afraid of a connection between them but that he was jealous of their friendship with her that not too long ago he had held so dear.

Francis had shown his naiveté, because that's what he wanted, by believing he might be able to salvage a friendship from the very abrupt end to their relationship. The complications were bound to surface as it was too soon. Francis thought that it was possible but Gem was dealing with the facts. Those cold stony facts dreamers love to ignore. Herman wished to give the dreamer a distraction and suggested that he partake in one of the games, thinking it would keep his mind off the subject.

"I thought you said they're dangerous."

"Well yes but we should be able to start you on a sport with less contact, to see how you fare. What you think, up for it?"

"Jesus, yeah for sure," Francis replied, without even having to think.

"Ok meet me at the left side of the main stand in fifteen minutes for back bowling."

"Back bowling," he yelped.

"You'll love it," he shouted as he scurried off into the crowd.

Moments later Francis had informed Alex of the invitation from Herman to participate in one of the games.

"You're such a lucky bastard!"

She had witnessed him do incredible things the last two days as well as seeing him so worried and sad. She was sincerely delighted for him.

"That sounds fun, can I watch?" she asked.

Nodding his head in excitement, they both headed off in the direction of the bowling area. They had to pass in front of the main stand that was overflowing with spectators. As they approached the Back bowling it appeared there was also a very large group surrounding it. Screams and shouts of names that meant nothing to Francis or Alex could be heard. Then, without warning, a sapphire stone emerged from the creatures. "You're down for the bowling Francis follow me please."

"Oh, I thought that was it," he replied.

"No that's the pro section. You're a beginner and that's the next section along."

The beginner section was nearly at the end of the stand and it got hardly any attention, which was probably better for Francis as he had no idea what to expect. Twenty or so spectators were standing there watching a few players. Their calls for the next player were drowned out by the incessant shouting from one of the pro sections.

Francis' pace quickened as a player made ready to take an attempt with what looked like a bowling ball. The creature ran forward, stopped at the line and let it go. The ball ran straight along the level ground at a ridiculously fast speed in the direction of a mound of sand that arched up into the shape of a huge wave. It was more like a frozen wave; the crest appeared to hang in mid air. *How could that be?* Francis thought. As the ball hit the base of the wave, it slowed a little then reached the top and returned into the air back to the creature that had tossed it.

The creature had taken what resembled a baseball bat from its other hand. The ball was coming back as an easy ball Francis might give his sister to be nice. The creature swung hard and caught the underside forcing the ball off to the left. It was a "miss hit" in baseball terms but had some power. Leaving a trail of smoke and sparks, it sped thought the air. Some distance away it exploded with a bang and flash of light.

Francis immediately started asking the official questions regarding the game. He was pushy to try, and was quietly confident as he was a good batsman on the school team. There was a line of three players and Francis was gestured to join the line. The next player missed the ball while the second hit a cracker of a strike causing a loud bang. The spectators loved the explosion two hundred feet away which got a cheer from a small section of the stand. The pro section beside them was so packed that play was hidden from sight. You knew someone had tossed the ball by the reaction of the creatures giving what sounded like a Mexican wave and abruptly fell silent as the ball came back over the top of the crowd. The strike from the unseen player produced a massive bang and the stone shot off into the sky. Upon reaching the sea, it exploded with a thunderous noise, sending fireworks in every direction. Orange, red and yellow streamers raced from the centre. Screaming fans went wild, jumping into the air chanting any sort of inaudible words. It was as if Liverpool had scored the winner against Manchester United in the champion's league final. *If only,* Francis thought.

The official explained to Francis the use of the bat but he wasn't listening. He then placed the ball, a sunstone, into his hands.

"The stone has been altered by magic to hold together and will explode brighter, depending on the quality of the strike," the official said.

Francis suddenly stepped sideways away from him and let the ball fly. Immediately the creature ran for cover and so did the few standing on the sideline.

"Shit," Francis said. Quickly realising the stone was heading right back to him.

Unknown to Francis, a number of spectators in the stand had been watching everything as no human had ever played this before. He had three seconds to ready himself. He swung, aiming high for there was nothing else to do. He sliced it, but hard.

To Francis it appeared that the sunstone had exploded before him. It hadn't!! As soon as he hit it, he fell sideways to the ground. Smoke trailed away towards the wave crest of the pro section. It passed right through leaving a gaping hole at an incredible speed in the direction of the centre arena. When it exploded about three hundred feet away, Francis was still stumbling around.

Some fifty feet above the ground there was a monstrous, thunderous explosion. Every single competitor beneath were tossed to the ground flat. Sand rose up and fell like rain onto everyone below.

For a moment there was silence. The spectators from the pro area had turned around as soon as they heard the bat hitting the stone. Many had ducked to take cover fearing the ball may strike them. Shocked to see a human had hit it. The blast was incredible even at two hundred meters. The destruction on the playing field was insane. About a thousand creatures were affected. Spectators in the stand were screaming, "Landmine! Landmine!" and loving it.

The scene at the centre of the field was very different. Hundreds of creatures were picking themselves up out of the sand. The hole was massive. They were blown in every direction by the force. Most had been flattened into the sand. Thankfully, no-one was seriously injured.

Instantly stones and crabs alike were trying to talk to Francis but he had been deafened by the noise upon hitting the sunstone and had no idea what he had done. A vain attempt to show that his hearing was suffering from the shock, pointing to his ears he made no sense to them.

The creatures loved that Francis was really unconcerned by what had happened. Many creatures looking back from the playing field towards the stand were surrounded by falling sand and sparks. Not to mention the cloud of smoke already covering the entire pitch. *Francis, Francis what have you done?* he whispered in his mind.

His mouth dropped open when he discovered what happened. *Holy shit! I didn't do that? Did I?* he asked himself. Around him creatures were screaming, "Landmine!"

From the stand it looked incredible. Even though only a very small section had heard the strike. Many more from the corner of their eyes saw the sunstone racing like a bullet through the air above creatures that appeared so tiny in the distance from the great stand. Seeing this they were now expecting craziness. No-one was disappointed.

It took ages for the commotion to end. Around fifteen minutes later, small sections of the stand were continuing to scream for "Landmine" to take another shot. Francis was being forced into it. He was told nobody was injured so when he finally agreed everyone applauded. Not because he was so good, but rather because of the reckless destruction his first shot had caused. They had not finished filling the hole on the pitch when he walked up to the line. About one hundred spectators were giving him a wide berth for his swing.

"I haven't played in a while," he said glancing back towards the crowd who were a little concerned. He let fly the ball but noticed that as it went up the wave of sand it didn't slow and was returning too high as it sped past his head into the wall of sand behind. The stand gave a respectful clap.

Francis' disappointment was clear. Pointing to the wave suggesting it was at fault, not his talent. He was quickly given another sunstone. This he tossed slower hoping to receive a different return. This time he was afraid of the ball and avoided the shot completely, letting it slam into the sand again. Everyone must have been thinking one-shot-wonder as clearly they were not happy.

"I love baseball," he whispered. Francis reached for his shades. Placing them over his eyes, he took a slow, deep breath. Being that protected from everyone's stare helped him immensely. He held the sunstone up to his mouth with both hands and kissed it while his mind was licking it. Similar to ways he had licked another stone at home in bed. As he lowered it into position he rubbed it against his cheek. Suddenly he felt a connection. Like he had kissed another stone, no many stones over the years and then let it fly. This got quite a few of the crowd talking. The return was perfectly placed above the hip. With a thunderous crack, Francis knocked it for six, for an instance blinding the few hundred directly on the sideline. Francis stumbled, unbalanced for a moment. The sunstone shot into the air in the direction of the ocean. Blazing fourth like a Soyuz Rocket taxi reaching for space but it didn't seem to stop.

Normally the sunstones exploded after a few hundred metres but it was way past a mile and still climbing over the ocean. Nobody in the stand could avoid the sight. It looked spectacular. A flash resembling a neutron bomb lit up the sky. Two seconds later the noise reached the beach. It was the very fabric of the atmosphere ripping apart to the complete joy of every creature present. The stand went wild, falling over each other in jubilation at seeing such a sight they leapt onto the beach from the lower stand like a landslide engulfing a tiny village at the base of a mountain. Francis was beaming from ear to ear.

"Damn that feels good!" he said raising his head.

Pushing his way past the creatures surrounding him, he grabbed another sunstone from the basket and tossed it towards the wave like a giddy child. Everyone who witnessed what was happening stepped backwards. Swinging within a small circle it was a miracle he completely missed their heads which were inches beyond the reach of his bat as he swung. Shocked expressions on the faces of many creatures turned to excitement when they saw what he was doing. Smashing the stone head on. Again the stone blasted off into the sky in the direction of the shoreline. Nobody could avoid the blinding flash including Francis, even with shades but it didn't matter as they loved it.

He fell to the ground laughing, a little overcome by the eagerness and the two beers he had drunk. The sunstone roared over the heads of other competitors in the middle of their games and exploded off shore. Although it didn't have the same beautiful light show of the previous shot, it sent a wave rushing towards the beach that caused a panic on the shoreline that sent hundreds running to higher ground.

Smasher was already making his way under orders of Herman to rescue Francis from his new supporters. When he arrived, Francis was being treated like a rock star. He pushed his way in and hoisted him as gently as he could above everyone and left. Smasher made his way to the water front and dropped him into the sea to try and sober him up.

From under the water jumped a very different Francis. Disconnected and angry he was ranting foul words at what he considered to be abuse and mistreatment. Dripping wet he was screaming, but soon understood it was for his own good.

"Water! Water! I need some water!" he shouted.

Smasher stood far taller than Francis but still managed to rest a soft touch onto his shoulder with his massive hand to help him up the beach. Smasher had placed both his feet in the water but was fortunate to possess the great strength to step out again. Other smaller creatures would not dare place an inch of their bodies into the water for fear of getting stuck.

Francis arrived at a watering hole of sorts where fresh water was available for the competitors. He took one of the buckets and poured it over his head, drinking as it flowed over his face. He reached for another taking his fill, having been dehydrated from the beers he had drunk and the blistering heat. It was 38 degrees and he felt quite faint. The water was helping sober him up to some extent.

"Coffee, I need coffee," he said next.

"Neva is the only one who can help you with that, Francis," Smasher answered in a sympathetic tone. Smasher had never been drunk but understood what it looked like as every human had drunk beer at Neva's. He knew it helped them relax, reminding them of home.

"Where does he get it all from Smasher?" Francis asked as he nearly tripped over himself.

Pausing in thought Smasher had no real answer.

"He never leaves the beach so someone must deliver it, I suppose."

Squinting his eyes while rubbing his nose with his index finger. "Must have good connections." Francis suggested.

"Yeah, must have."

Chapter Nineteen

CALM BEFORE THE STORM

Francis carried the bucket to The Cock Traven. Drinking as he walked though it looked rather funny as he spilled five times the amount that actually went into his mouth. Francis received many looks from creatures that knew he was responsible for the sunstone explosions. He was delighted and showed it by smiling back at them. It was the feeling of being accepted that Smasher recognised. He had seen many creatures play games over the years and have great success. Herman's idea was working, for the most part.

Reaching the pub there was a large enough gathering enjoying the extra energy and enthusiasm sweeping about the beach. The games, the fact that everyone's appearance had completely changed. *Beautiful* and *clean* quickly became two new buzz words. Three granite blocks approached to congratulate Francis for his achievement. Francis took it in his stride and started explaining how strange it was to be tossed into a great game and admit he loved it. Alex arrived and slapped him a low five.

"That was amazing bro!" she raved.

"I know. What a fucking crazy game. I LOVE it. Can't wait to do it again. And before you say it, yes I am so relieved no-one was hurt."

"Yeah, those stones are pretty tough. But you have skill, it always helps hey."

Neva shouted, "Coming through! Coming through!"

Instantly the many spectators pulled back to let him pass. He reached for Francis' hand gripping it tight. Francis was very much the centre of attention.

"Welcome to the club!" he shouted turning to his new audience, who all cheered. "Please come up to the bar for a drink."

"He seems to be dehydrated, Neva," Smasher explained.

"No worries mate. I will look after him. I know exactly what he needs."

"Francis, I'm going back to the games, Herman needs to talk to you and Alex before you return home later so please wait for him," Smasher stressed

"Thanks Smasher, we will," Francis waved good-bye.

Neva was very excited and knew Francis couldn't have played that game without magic, so was frank with his next statement.

"Whatever you're peddling I want in. Maybe we can sell it? We need a marketing gimmick. I loved landmine and depth charge. We're going to make a FORTUNE!"

"Neva, you know I think you're more human than stone."

"Well, that's not untrue. Let's be honest, it's more fun, and I know there are already drinks with those names in your world. But the beach is like China, no copyright laws."

While Neva continued with his ideas of making millions, the same two human girls from a few days ago approached the bar. Too busy with his own thoughts then, Francis had said almost nothing to them. This time, Francis was much more open to conversation. He found himself quite at home talking to them both about the events of the day. Olive was from Kenya, her friend, Maria, from Sweden. Both were members of a secret organisation for student witches back home. Francis found the conversation fascinating learning all he could. He told the girls that he and his sister had been given permission from an Irish witch to travel to the beach for research.

Alex was now sipping on a glass of wine; which was exactly the amount she was allowed to drink at the Christmas dinner table. The others were drinking their fill. Francis was still on the water.

Maria asked the name of the witch, Francis said Eloïse. She looked at Olive in a way that Francis understood they knew her, but the questionable expression on her face left him thinking. After noticing this he decided it would be better to pretended to be more in the know regarding her.

"She's a crazy bitch, sorry witch, but she has done great things over the years." He smiled.

Hearing this, Maria immediately spat out a mouthful of beer she was swallowing onto the sand laughing. Quickly, she wiped her mouth and apologised for her actions. She was so embarrassed. Alex listened intensely to everything.

After a long pause, Maria started to talk in a lower tone. Francis and Alex got the impression both girls were in fear of something regarding Eloïse.

"Well, you're right there. She has always been a bit of a renegade." She paused looking at Francis who was playing it cool and letting her talk.

"How well do you know her?" she asked very politely.

"Well enough for her to let us come here, and I think she is helping us, me."

"That's rich considering her past," Olive explained.

"Yeah, you're right there," Francis responded perfectly. "At least she didn't start that way. That's what I think," he added, as if feeling sorry for her.

This line of answers was having a positive effect on the girls and made them both relax. They were amazed at hearing they had a candle repeatedly asking to see it. In the end, Alex gave them a quick glance into her bag but no touching allowed. The girls said nothing to this as they understood how valuable it was.

The girls joked about where they would travel and what to see if they had a device like that for a few days. After what seemed ages Alex returned to the subject of Eloïse saying that herself and Francis felt so lucky to have witnessed so much, experienced things the rest of the world knew nothing of. The girls felt the same but were happy that they would be able to accomplish so much good back home. Several times they had pointed out that the witches and wizards of the world were, for the most part, keeping it together and safe.

Alex enjoyed getting the background information, given how little they knew of the normal goings-on. Although they had been privilege to some of the most important creatures and information unknown to mankind in a very short time.

Francis and Maria were happily talking together and drifted into a more private conversation nearer to the bar. She was very curious as to why they were both on the beach. It was extremely rare to find humans that weren't wizards or witches in this world.

"Before lunch today we were all told to return to the inn at the far end of the beach because some crazy invisible nutcase had killed some crabs. I love this place but I've never take off my bracelet, even when sleeping. I also heard that a stone brought from our world transformed into a girl and that there is some kind of showdown coming, involving lots of the big names on the beach. We might have to leave but I know the magic in the bracelet will protect me mostly . . . and well it's not that I don't know a few tricks."

"Yeah, I know," Francis answered with a very respectful tone. "Two weeks ago I didn't know this place existed, Maria. Now I am completely in love with it."

"Not surprising if you keep hitting sunstones like that."

"You saw that?" he enquired.

"Francis, everyone saw that! You must have pretty important friends even to be let play in the games. Not to mention magic. I am sure you understand how dangerous it is."

"Well, yeah, I have been a bit lucky I think." Francis avoided any conversation regarding the story behind his party tricks, but happily told her about their new friends Herman and Smasher. Eventually, she got the story about Gem but was a little shocked to discover she had been a stone - not the normal dating partner for a human. But a moment later she understood that the stone he had been with was the one the trouble was about. Francis made it very clear that they were no longer together. Bending forward, he kissed her on the cheek. Maria was fine with this and suggested that she get the next round.

"Francis, sorry when I say get the next round in Sweden, it means paying for it with cash. I have never paid for anything on the beach. That's a bit strange?"

"I know what you mean. I have been wondering where they get the supplies for us."

"Have you seen the guesthouse?" she asked.

"No,"

"God, it's beautiful. Every morning you get a full breakfast with fresh orange juice."

"Don't tell my sister that," they both laughed.

As they continued talking Francis started drinking beer again and was feeling the effects of the alcohol as he hadn't eaten yet today. He was not in the mood to talk about Gem and had wished Maria would let it go. His emotions were running high and strong feelings were racing through his mind, when in the corner of his eye Gem appeared. Maria was still talking to him. Francis kept nodding his head but had stopped listening. She hadn't notice at first; his mind was on other matters. Turning around, she saw the reason walking through the crowd. Gem could no longer be compared to a stone from the outside. You could only see a beautiful young woman. Of course nothing could be further from the truth regarding her state of mind. Like Francis she was experiencing great difficulty right now in her long life. For a moment, Francis rummaged in his pocket looking for a stone but, of course, found none.

His brain raced back to his bedroom and started showing images of him licking it under the covers. Had he lost his mind? No, he was lusting after what he no longer had access to. Call it a friendship, a relationship or a drug. He missed it and therefore was trapped in its nightmare. The drinks had now taken him over the edge. He was in a very courageous mood and started walking away from the bar towards her. Passing by some tables bumping into a few creatures he apologised as best he could for knocking over their drinks. As he continued walking words flashed before his eyes over and over. He was rehearsing what he was going to say, repeating his understanding viewpoint and anger at how she had been treating him. Then abruptly forgetting it and starting from scratch again.

"Shit, I've already forgotten what I wanted to say, damn," he mumbled. Three seconds later, he was standing in front of her. She turned away and started walking in the opposite direction from the group.

"Gem," Francis shouted at her, losing patience. "I wanted to tell you something."

"Francis, leave me alone. I have so much going on." She tossed a glance to heaven shaking her head, showing openly her discomfort at talking to him.

"I heard everything and I know what's happening."

"You don't know shit, Francis."

"Why won't you talk to me? What's the fucking problem?" he pleaded.

"You are, Francis. I heard you were talking about us to everyone. Forget you and me. If you discuss our business with anyone else, I will finish you."

"What about you and me being friends?" his heart was racing.

"You will be part of my life when I say it. Not when you want. Ok?" she shouted

Those words rang deep in his mind. Everything around slowed down. He walked for a moment wanting to sit down. He was furious, about to vomit, his stomach was grinding. Tears raced down his face as he completely failed to understand what was happening. The way it always happens with emotions that rule young hearts and as such controlled Francis' every decision.

"Bitch," he said as he wiped his face. Reaching for a bowl of water on the table he tossed it onto his face. There was a burning sensation inside his head.

"Fuck this shit!" he stood up and wiped his eyes.

Francis was visualising a terrible nightmare. Something so full of vengeance, malice, it was definitely considered revenge. Around his feet, the sand started vibrating. Pop! Pop! Two little heads from the island he had visited in his mind during the meeting with Sandstones appeared beside his feet. Their swollen, dark, lonely eyes sank away into the ground till nothing of their shape was left. Francis shook his head. He was uncertain if he was starting to imagine things that weren't there. If anything, he understood the sadness in their eyes.

He raised himself and walked back to the girls, hiding the tears but shaking his head. Stretching his arms into the air, he shouted with delight, "The Cock Tavern!"

Francis was reacting to the situation the same way people had done for thousands of years. There was nothing unusual about it except that it was from his point of view as an individual. He despised Gem. That was, of course, absolutely normal. He never had the time to tell Gem he wasn't talking to everyone about them, or their business. Herman and Smasher had expressed great interest in helping him. He had to talk to somebody. Everyone wanted to help her at the moment because of the situation with José. He may have been slightly immature, but he deserved an answer from her. Not the behaviour she had shown him of late.

The jealousy he felt toward his friends seeing her more than him turned on and off like the flick of a switch; he thought about what a stone was. How hard, lifeless and void of feeling. She was nothing but a stone until he gave her his feelings. The fact that she didn't want to see him even as a friend was very confusing. The spell was a terrible trick for any living creature to endure. She might have dumped him because she wanted to protect him or herself from going too far, as she had done that before and lost everything. Who knows? He thought. But probably she had absolutely no control over anything.

"What kind of a crazy bitch was I going out with in the first place? Now that I think about it. I should have seen the signs from the fucking beginning. So what? I was in love because I was blind to her shit. Or I needed something so mad, so messed up, wacky, not of this earth." He stopped dead in his tracks and whispered, "the beach."

Returning to the girls, there was a more positive stride to his manner.

Francis noticed that Alex was missing. Olive handed over Alex's bag. Saying she needed to go talk to a crab called Eric.

"Cheers, no worries," he took the bag back.

"Shouldn't you be a little worried, Francis? I know you're hanging out with crabs but we were also warned not to trust them. I did try to stop her."

"She'll be fine. He's a great guy. Can you excuse me for a moment girls? I'll be right back."

Francis walked off. Reaching into her bag, he removed a small pocket knife. He then took the candle and started peeling off the top till there was hardly anything left of the colour red. He knew exactly what he wanted. It didn't help that he was a little drunk and running on emotions. Making rash decisions seemed right. Doing it alone was the correct way.

When finished, he returned to The Cock Traven. Heading back to the guesthouse, the girls said goodbye. He was hoping to see them again soon as Maria was sweet.

Two hours later Herman, Smasher, Eric, Francis and Alex sat together safe within the walls of Smasher's house. Francis was now relaxed. He had a plan that didn't involve talking to Gem. Drinking lots of water since they had left The Cock Tavern also helped. He was sober and very capable of understanding what was happening. Herman had informed them that José would make his final strike in the next two days, before the end of the games. He was not content with taking Gem, but was planning to cause as much death and destruction in front of everyone, a reminder of what was committed upon him many years ago. The situation was extremely dangerous to say the least. Herman admitted it was now impossible to kill him. The best choice was to magically freeze him somehow and dump him into the deepest trench for eternity. Francis had agreed to assist in whatever way he could with his newfound skill.

Francis and Alex said their goodbyes and were led to the door. Walking down the street the conversation was nothing to laugh about.

"Do you think you can kill him Francis?" she asked.

"Don't know." His mind was clearly on other matters. Francis was not making sense and Alex was a little worried for him. She understood the implications of what had happened regarding Gem.

"Are you listening? What are we going to do?" She tugged on his t-shirt.

He was still carrying her bag and reached to get the candle as they were at what appeared as good a spot as any for their departure. Lighting it, he placed it on the ground so Alex would not notice what he had done. Slowly the circle of light grew to about the usual two metres in every direction. The walls of their house started to appear around them. Then Francis abruptly walked out of the light as he had done many times; for living matter this was like walking under water as the two worlds mixed.

"Come on you have too many stones in your bedroom already. Francis, if anyone from the beach sees exactly how many, they are sure to think you have mental health issues," she said smiling.

He picked up a large stone and turned to Alex from the other side of the light.

"Come on. Quickly," she said. Francis didn't move, staring straight at her. Alex didn't seem to understand what was happening.

"Francis, will you hurry up! Come on. What are you doing?" There was a sudden taste of dread in her words. She screamed as he tossed the stone in the direction of the candle, it passed straight through the light barrier and SMACK! Knocked it over.

Alex, the candle, and the light vanished instantly.

Chapter Twenty
END GAME

Francis sat by himself weeping uncontrollably. He knew what he had done was terrible. His sister would probably never forgive him. The expression of horror on her face just before she disappeared was too much for him to bear.

Herman and Smasher were beside themselves with worry for him. They had become such good friends.

Also Eloïse had no idea how it would play out. She had used them both but never wanting to hurt them, although she knew it would be dangerous letting two humans loose on the beach. She had made certain they would be provided with magical charms to protect and guide them both. But Alex and Francis had received the help from the very creatures she had advised them to avoid. She also knew they would both undergo great changes the longer they spent on the beach.

That's life. Everyone grows up at some stage. Herman had no means to send him back to his world right now, even if he wanted to return. In many way, Francis had experienced madness and survived. His brief encounter with Gem had nearly ruined him, in the very same manner she had been destroyed by José. He hadn't played any relationship game and lost, because he couldn't tell if he was playing a game of any kind with Gem. For the last number of days he had awoken thinking about her. Over and over nothing made sense and he survived because he had friends to turn to, that along with a few crazy events surrounding him helped with distracting his worrisome thoughts.

Talking and getting things out in the open was always better. Herman had helped Francis with solid conversation. José never had that chance. He, on the other hand, had gone completely insane from having so much control over Gem and never setting her free. But his story was the same, with regard to having been given a stone. José found Gem in the same form Francis did, because a person made that happen all that time ago.

Everyone who ever loved or lusted after somebody went through that at some level. Francis was unable to hide his emotions so soon. What would he do now? Alex and Francis had experienced so much, living a dream. That she had returned home added to the reasons the world appeared to be collapsing around him.

On one side, they had found Sandstone, the most interesting creature ever to live who had not been seen for hundreds, maybe thousands of years. The story of the golden wall had made Francis cry with joy because he understood how much of a big deal that was. The Church keeping that from everyone was a mistake. He would dream about seeing it for the rest of his life. Aliens on earth! Finding out that Jesus was a real living person was amazing, too.

The icing on the cake was in discovering that Jesus had another name, possibly his real name, in a language no human had heard before was unbelievable, literally it was beyond belief that Francis knew this name changed everything. He held the recklessness of a young boy who was at a turning point in his life. Herman and Smasher considered him very dangerous because he was human and unpredictable. Was this part of the plan? Was Eloïse behind this? He simply didn't care at the moment.

Herman approached Francis as a mother would her child. He had a lifetime of experience. Most important was his timing for compassion. He had seen wonders that boggled the mind, actions from individuals that would shock anyone, even a creature from the beach but he had no proper answer for love.

"Francis, what am I?" he asked as softly a crab could.

"You're a crab," Francis responded as if replying to his maths teacher.

"Yes we know you call us crustaceans and we live in the sea, Francis." Herman's eyes reached for the sky and nearly made it.

"Well, that's it. You evolved over millions of years into what you are today. Like all mankind."

"Yes, we know that, but where did we come from, Francis? Can you answer that? Because I want to know the name of that place."

"Space!" Francis blurted out, after a long pause.

Sensing that he needed another approach, Herman started again.

"You know I can't believe that you've got as far as you have. I am willing to bet it has to do with the type of person you are. I have liked you since the very first moment we met. I'm not saying that to make you feel better. Look at me, covered in magical rings and I never saw this coming. The longer you were with Gem the more of yourself you saw in her. I know realise this. From seeing you over the last week I understand how you manage your brain."

"You've been watching my brain?!" Francis stated, as he pulled his shoulders back taking a deep breath.

Herman smiled at that.

"Humans give off; what you call a vibe. Your heart is in the right place, even thought you use it as your brain in situations you shouldn't. But that's what you're here for, Francis. Isn't it?"

"I'm listening, please continue."

"Over the years I have seen much of your kind. Lazy, upbeat, studious, mad, stuck-up, messed up and that's the reason mankind is so much fun. You're so completely different. It's a matter of fact that we have on the beach one crazy crab! one and look how bad it is. He tormented her to get what he wanted. He used her for his own perverse reasons. He kept her interested in a cruel way. Made her feel that she needed help, put her down, patronize her. The list is endless. She was afraid and would never admit it because she knew no better in the end. He left her thinking the relationship could be over tomorrow. That's why she held onto him even tighter. I was there when she introduced you to Neva and well, it was very obvious she was looking for approval. Francis, she is a *stone*! Nothing more. Look about you. There are millions on this beach alone. The changes happening to you will mark you as a man. I know that because I've seen it many times. Sure, ten years ago I got together with this crazy crab from the low rock. It's about a mile that way," he raised his left claw and pointed out to sea. "Completely nuts but it made me feel great for a while. She changed after about three months. I saw the real her. But I was dating another girl at the same time so didn't get too upset."

"Hold on a moment. You were two-timing? Well, that's fucking brilliant. A crab giving me advice and he's screwing half the beach?!"

"Wait a moment, Francis! I certainly wasn't using anyone. They were friends nothing more. You humans always rush things along. But I know you have very little control over that. You had the stone, sorry Gem, for a week. But it felt like six months. That's because you put so much into it, Francis. She didn't have to as she saw you were doing the work. It was the other way round for her and José. She did all the work. She was punished and pushed over the edge by him."

"I get you, Herman. I mean the part that she is a stone," Francis replied.

"I don't think you do, Francis, because people throw stones into the water when they're thinking of something else, if you get me. And while she won't talk to you, it makes matters worse as you have no idea what's on her mind. You have reached the abyss, the end of the road," he said, his voice raised.

"She's worse than a damn reflection stone. José treated her like a tramp, and in return she was a goddess to him. You treated her like a goddess and she treated you like rubbish. She's caused you more trouble than she's worth. Believe me when I say that. She is the pendant on a necklace that a princess would hang around her neck for a grand ball in Vienna for one night, and then lock away in a safe for the following year, Francis. It's wonderful to see her again because as a stone I admire her. But between you and me, she's a bitch as a human being. Why is she? I will remind you again," he carried on.

"José made her into one, Francis, and that's simply the way it is. She is in the wrong place at the wrong time," he paused, "and I am sure not by her own doing. Not you, Francis. She is interrupting your life. You haven't stopped hers. I know you see the bigger picture."

Suddenly Herman stood up as best a crab three inches tall can.

"My wish, regardless of the outcome, is that you never change, my friend."

There was a long moment of silence. Francis looked down to Herman, with an expression of gratitude and content he started to stand.

"Let's go finish José."

As they walked Herman talked about life's journey. Being a dreamer, Francis was always quicker to see many of the possible different outcomes before the average person could. Listening to Herman was like stepping into a doorway he had never passed through before.

"It's a road and you're on it. Seeing into the distance your dreams and such- like ahead of you," he said.

Francis' mind saw this road of life and his mind imagined it looked like parked cars on the pavement as he drove by on a busy motorway. They must be the ones that broke down and were never repaired, or perhaps had a flat tyre. An unlucky moment in your life like losing your job. To the left the car park was so vast it was impossible to see its end. It was glittering in the sun like the panels from a massive solar farm in a land with no trees. Far off in the distance, you could see the odd one on fire. *God I hope no body is hurt,* he thought as one exploded. A black cloud raced into the sky. Francis was focused on this one point. He could see people running towards it and a fight between a couple of men. There was many standing around watching it happen. *Unbelievable,* he thought. *Unbelievable! Those bastards look at them. Bastards!! It's pathetic.*

They both continued walking along with their own thoughts but well aware they would use Gem to bring José out into the open. Most of the work would be done by the crabs and a small group of stones who knew of the plan. Herman would lead after it had started. When they were in the mill of things the combined might of a few thousand solider crabs channelling their magic through Herman would finish the job. "The killing" as they called it, was another name for turning him into a stone enabling them to cast him to the bottom of the ocean forever.

As they walked Francis talked of many things to Herman. Putting on his shades he felt well-adjusted to the hot days and freezing nights.

"I love the beach Herman. I love this place. I feel I have a connection with it," pausing a moment, "no, I have youth and emotions to offer it, Herman. You and the other creatures of the beach have changed me. It's hard to explain but I feel very different."

"What?" Herman asked as he scurried forward looking up to him.

"The games bring out a remarkable special closeness, a feeling of togetherness that the beach is lacking from a few days back. Its nuts but I like the way you play out your lives on the beach. I mean you choose your times well, because you're so old."

"Thank you, Francis," Herman replied sincerely. "I am afraid that's exactly right, and you came to that conclusion in a week on your own! That's fantastic."

Herman stood staring at him for a moment. "You're not overly worried about getting back home, Francis, and that's a little unsettling. It's your business but I know it's upsetting you regarding your sister. I will be able to get you home eventually, but not until after the business with José is sorted."

"Oh that's ok, Herman. I have the feeling that Eloïse will soon be arriving on the beach to check in as she would be very unhappy with how I left Alex. She made a leap of faith allowing Alex and I to travel here alone. But I am so happy, that she did. Alex, I am sure is with her right now explaining everything that happened over the last few days. But that's not going to stop me."

"Stop you?" Herman looked slightly concerned. "Stop you from doing what exactly, Francis?"

"Oh something I have been pondering."

Francis didn't notice the slight change in his expression. Francis lowered his hand and Herman leaped onto it. Walking faster it seemed a great journey was drawing to a close. Maybe the great mountain range of the Himalayas had also finally reached that conclusion in the end. They could be pushed no further to heaven. Millions of years could pass by as they crumbled and collapsed. To be churned up by the earth and reform on the other side of the world. How dark and cold it must be to be in that place.

Herman knew Francis was much more relaxed and confident, not afraid to discuss any subject. It's as if he was seeing Francis reflect on his life. Understanding his mistakes and what direction he would go in next. They also discussed how Gem would be transformed back into a stone temporarily to lure José.

"He will expect a trap; spells will be in place surrounding her. But enough to keep him interested. He knows nothing of your heart, Francis, and that's where we have him."

Herman was expecting José to do a show. He already won the first confrontation so he will be expecting another victory.

"He is using his magic as raw power, Francis. Like a bulldozer pushing down a house. There is no style or cunning in his ability. He will expect us to charge with a full frontal attack. You, my friend, will simply blindside him."

"Then Herman he's in for a huge surprise!"

Chapter Twenty-One

BATTLE

At exactly 5.15p.m. José arrived, dressed in black. As he walked, his rings of white gold reflected off his neck. The light formed a circle resembling the white collar of a priest. It was like evil dressed in uniform. The head honcho was dripping revenge onto the hot sand. He walked with such contempt that never in his wildest dreams could he have imagined what was going to happen next. It would be akin to asking the Pope if he thought Jesus was right to smash up the stands of the gamblers and criminals in the temple and, if he was to return tomorrow, what did he imagine he would smash up nowadays?

Gem, who had transformed back into a small stone, was lying on the sand posing like a piece of cheese for a mouse. Close to her José very discreetly became visible. Most didn't notice until it was too late. So, once again, everyone within range had been frozen. Many still in mid-run, others facing another direction as they were unaware he was passing by behind them.

José intended to hold Gem for all eternity, to use and abuse her like a slave for his desires. He glanced left to right, a warrior surveying his future subjects from his throne. He was rolling his right claw around effortlessly above his eyes. Gem was motionless as a stone, which was part of the plan. But also to protect and hide her thoughts from him.

As agreed with Herman, Francis was standing a good distance away outside the perimeter of the spell. The word 'megalomaniac' jumped into everyone's head concerning José. Even though nobody could move, all eyes were on José. He paused to take a long stare in the direction of Herman who was completely powerless to oppose him.

"*Not nice,* seeing you again brother!" he shouted, While turning about laughing, he took his time at tossing out obscenities to the inhabitants of the beach. He was determined to leave nothing out. From instances of minor importance such as their arrogance, to the major efforts they had taken to evict him from the beach the last time. Again, he stopped. For a moment he was lost in thought as if he was searching for a meaningful phrase then forgot it and was desperately trying to retrieve it from the small brain he had been born with. Swallowing his pride he became aware everyone was staring at him. His ego although controlling him, had its limits. It was assumed that this behaviour was insanity.

"You make me sick," he shouted. "Sick, I tell you! Sick to the claws." He turned and pointed out to sea. "You're the reason I spent so long in that ocean. I should crush you for introducing me to her in the first place. Granite, Basalt, Gypsum, oh and let's not forget Sandstone and that stinking human witch Eloïse. The fucking bitch. What?! Nobody tell her I was back. Well, if she shows up I'll take her head off."

Screaming with rage, he smashed his left claw into the sand. As the sand flew through the air it ignited and fell upon the creatures nearer to him. It burnt everything that it touched causing terrible pain.

Herman was waiting for the chance. Although he hated the fact creatures were being hurt he could stand it for the moment but if José went further he would spring the trap. Herman had no time to even consider how better the world would be without one of his brothers. In the past, he had tried to help on numerous occasions but he would do almost anything to send him to the bottom of the ocean today. He knew that José would forget everything and slowly lose shape and return to sand. Herman's legs started twitching. Someone in the surrounding crowd started to speak. Herman couldn't immediately identify who was talking but when he saw Francis walking forward he was terrified.

"Excuse me," Francis said. His mind was having serious trouble trying to comprehend what he heard a moment ago. "You know of Eloïse? How is that?"

Thousands of reasons as to how flowed through his mind. Every single frozen creature's eyes veered in his direction with total shock. Who could possibly be that insane, as to interrupt José in such a moment of madness.

"Sorry. You said you know Eloïse? Well, so do I," his voice was raised. "She introduced me to Gem not so long ago. I am very curious to know why she did."

This was not part of the plan they agreed to earlier and surely would end badly.

"What the hell is going on?" he stared confidently down at José. Then, turning to Herman his expression changed to anger. Herman was unable to hold back his fear and slowly started to chant his spell.

"Francis! We have more important matters at hand. Please, I never knew," he shouted with the stress of a living meal trying to untie themselves from the dinner plate of a T-Rex.

There was silence. José in the meantime was busy trying to understand the questions and relevance of Francis. He was also confused as to why his spell had no effect on him. To the frozen creatures it was as if the music abruptly ended mid-song at an amazing dance party. The electricity was so intense the sand was rising off the beach into the air before their very eyes. José's head was tilted to the sky in thought. He turned to Herman then back to Francis.

Then suddenly it became clear. He understood Francis was the lover of Gem. His blood, if he had any, was boiling. Francis had one second to dodge the green lightning bolt blasted from José's claw as he dived to the ground. It would have killed him instantly. He rolled to the left covering his ears as the noise was deafening. After the second blast Francis came to his knees wanting to defend himself.

A second later every frozen creature surrounding them was free and started running. It was the charge of the light brigade. Trying to escape this onslaught of missed or deflected surges of power was impossible. José continued firing at everything. Smasher was keeping his distance as planned. Massive explosions left and right tossed unlucky stones in every direction. At this point, it was difficult to see anything as the light from the flashes was so bright. The air was filled with sand and black smoke. The heat was so intense it was turning the sand to glass in places. Francis dived to the ground and managed to direct the sand with his thoughts to form a shield around himself deflecting the energy bolts from José. Other creatures scrambled to take cover behind larger outcrops or boulders that were unfortunately scattered too far apart.

Herman was free and was the first to hit back with bolts of pure energy bursting from his claws which for the moment seemed a distraction for José making him snigger.

Francis' emotions were running wild. He was fighting for his life. He talked to the sand and it understood his command. A sandstorm of Francis' making battered the invisible force field José surrounded himself with. From above and below every opening seemed closed. Then the sand within the protection of the invisible wall was lashing against him with the force of a hurricane. Winds of over one hundred miles an hour lashed him from inside his protected sphere. With commanding confidence he turned to Herman. Then still showing arrogance and delight he dispatched two bolts of thundering coloured energy across the sand in his direction.

José was unable to stop himself from being dragged forward inch by inch to Francis. He was unable to withstand the furiousness of the wind cutting into his body like some carpenter using sand paper on a rough piece of wood. José was screaming with pain. His magical wall of protection fell to the ground. Herman unleashed another bolt of death in his direction. Furious, José managed to take the pain again then threw everything at Francis like he had invented the word 'madness'. Surprisingly Francis was managing to toss it right back which made José even angrier.

At that very moment the ground started to vibrate in every direction for forty feet. Thousands of solider crabs, common crabs, sea crabs, land crabs of every size and colour started to emerge with their rings clattering. In the beginning it sounded like an out of tune orchestra, however with every passing moment steadily it grew into a unified humming.

On discovering this trap, José lashed out at everything. Blasting anything surrounding him, killing everything he could. This gave Francis a moment to think. The skin on his fingers was falling off. The air around him was incredibly hot and his hair was starting to curl. He could feel it burning. At that moment Herman let it go on José. With the combined power of a small army of creatures he let fly a spell that would finish him. Francis was on his knees nearly crying with the pain.

A bolt of light shot from Herman's claw screeching through the air. The sustained beam lifted José off the ground. He was terrified. Again to everyone's shock he drew some hidden power and started pushing it back, and was able to lower himself to the ground. Francis tried to stand up but another blinding flash of light appeared to the left of him, but no explosion. Unable to see what it was, quickly he returned his gaze to José. When the dust settled a figure walked through the smoke. It was Eloïse.

Almost immediately both Francis and Herman heard a voice inside their heads. *I will explain everything later. I have come to help. Francis, keep burying him in sand. Herman and I will do the rest.* Within an instance of José seeing her, everything within a number of feet from his little body exploded outwards at a terrifying speed. Sand, rocks, crabs, flying through the air. Herman was still channelling the power from the remaining crabs and sent it pounding in Jose's direction again. Striking him in the upper part of a back leg like a bullet shattering a Chinese vase a section broke off splintered into tiny pieces. The pain was pushing José into over *kill* mode, but he still continued!

Eloïse was shouting a spell over the noise produced from the massive energies being assembled at the end of her fingertips. The sleeves on her cloak were pushed back, the very air around her body was vibrating. Through the flying sand and smoke Francis saw the outstretched hands of a young woman not an old witch. She was beautiful. Francis didn't think. He did exactly what she said. The sand that surrounded José started pulling towards him, making it almost impossible for him to see what was happening. José's frustration was incredible.

"You can't have her. She is mine. I own her. You hear me. I am going to kill every last one of you bastards. Eloïse you gave me her. She's mine. You bitch!" With that the sand around him started forming into large rocks, then shot through the air towards Eloïse. They shattered a short distance from her against an invisible wall of bullet-proof glass. Smash after smash they impacted causing large cracks. Many of the stones were even stuck in the shield. José was now totally loosing it.

"I will dispatch every living creature on this beach for my true love." he screamed with such savagery it physically hurt him.

Gem was lying on the beach like every other stone that had no means to move let alone escape. José himself was in no great shape. Dragging his left claw which appeared broken he had the appearance of surviving a nuclear explosion. Dazed, he retaliated one last time.

Herman drew every last drop of power he could to save his own life. Beams of orange light shot across the sand as if they were bullets from a machine gun. The energy encircling him was as if you were standing beside electric power lines as they buzzed in the rain. The rings on Herman's body started melting when the energy bolts struck him. Lying motionless on the sand, the silver liquid of his rings continued flowing over his body encasing him inside a protective shell.

Seeing this, José stopped firing. He was dizzy, confused and lost. Eloïse moved in for the kill. Francis lying flat on the ground instinctively knew the moment was right. He stuck his fingers into the sand and slowly wiggled them about to get a feel for it. Then with the flip of his index finger in the sand he sent a tiny wave towards José. As he watched it go forward, a large, dark shadow passed over his head. Looking up he saw the black silhouette of a giant creature passing above. José didn't see the wave of sand coming in his direction. He also didn't notice Smasher's large shape flying through the air. The wave calmly made its path across the sand, around other creatures and stones. Seconds later it flipped José on his back.

He rested thinking he could stay this way forever with the warm sun on his belly. But darkness was what he received as Smasher's fist hit him full force. He punched a hole four feet into the ground.

For a moment there was total silence. As the sand and dust blew away there came a short crack like when you step on a bathroom tile and it breaks. José's life as a crab was over.

Smasher reached into the hole quickly grabbing a handful of sand and dumped it onto the beach. There, half-covered in sand, the monster of the deep was motionless. Eloïse, Francis and Smasher stood beside him. For Eloïse it was a sad moment. She had seen such great potential in José, now forcefully destroyed.

Smasher on the other hand was smiling. To Francis the scene was familiar in many ways. A crab turned upside-down dead on a beach washed in by the tide back home. In the past, he might have said, "What had happened to the poor thing?" For a moment, he thought *my God, is this how all bad crabs come to their end?*

Eloïse raised her hand above José's broken body.

"What I am about to do means no return for him to the living." She started to chant. By degrees, José was transformed into stone, not too unlike the colour of the sand around him.

"Is it over?" Francis asked

"Yes," she replied.

Francis bent down, picked him up and placed him in his pocket next to another stone, one he had taken from the beach unnoticed by anyone during all the commotion. Their attention quickly returned to Herman. His entire body was covered in silver. Everything!! It was incredible to see. He was frozen with one claw held above his eyes, the other in a position of attack: a defining pose of courage and sacrifice. They felt profound sadness.

"I cannot lose him, Eloïse," Smasher said simply, without turning.

"Well, he's not dead, but you know that already. We will do our best. Understand, though, that I haven't a clue even where to start."

"Sandstone," Smasher suggested, "he won't be in the mood to talk to me when he discovers that I have been deceiving him."

Francis was trying to fill in the gaps; way too much was going on.

"Well, I can help you there, we get on great. I will do the talking to Sandstone Eloïse," Francis assured her.

"Yes, I can see your first conversation with him was a great success. You pack a punch with your dreaming," Eloïse replied.

Smasher very gently scooped up the sand beneath Herman and closed both his hands loosely around him, then proceeded to shake them and the tiny silver crab clattered around on the inside as the sand fell to the ground.

Once Smasher was assured all the sand had been removed, he opened his hands out flat and Herman was upside down. Smasher started to laugh, flicking Herman into the air with a short move of his stony palm he landed with a heavy metal clunk, upright!

Francis looked at Eloïse. Her dress was torn. The sleeves of her shirt were ripped on both arms. She was bleeding on her forehead and her hair was a mess. She seemed exhausted. Francis had forgotten his feelings of betrayal and helped her up the beach. He wasn't feeling too good himself, limping while his left hand was covered in his own blood. He understood his questions would be answered but not right now.

It was an incredible sight to behold. Francis imagined he was a soldier of fortune in a war that needed winning. He had a reason to fight in a far off land. His people had been oppressed for too long and finally they had won their freedom.

Everywhere he looked creatures received badly needed medical assistance. Hundreds of crabs had in the last few moments of the battle emerged from the ocean and were using their magic on the many injured. For the most part it was broken limbs as José was too busy to notice everyone working on his demise using magic under the sand, which helped save their lives because he couldn't see them at first. Some stones were being carried away and would need lots of attention having received deflected blasts of energy from the fight.

But they had done it and Francis was unable to hold in a smile. Tears of delight rolled down his face. It was amazing remembering the last few minutes. Eloïse was also extremely relieved at how this matter had ended.

"You were very brave, Francis. I knew you were special and I was right, for once."

As they approached The Cock Tavern it looked even more inviting than ever. Those huge table slabs were filled with creatures that had witnessed the final moments of José's life. Hermit crabs were looking for new homes because they were shattered by a blast of energy. Solider crabs were chatting with their buddies. A number of large sea crabs looking after lost baby fiddler crabs, and the most relaxed-looking king blue informing creatures where to look for friends or lost family members.

Everyone was in agreement this young human man had changed life forever on the beach. Smasher walked up to the centre stone of the bar. It was six feet high; far too tall for comfortable seating making it a perfect place for Herman at the moment. Everyone could see the crab that had helped to save them.

Chapter Twenty-Two

THE TRUTH

Francis handed Eloïse some water in a small stone cup. Then he stood there looking out over the beach with his hands in his pockets. He was rubbing Gem hard on her front; regardless of what she might be thinking, he liked it. He was dreaming away when the Master of Ceremonies came running up to the bar with two of his assistants.

"Everyone! Please listen!" he screamed.

This took awhile. The creatures were more concerned with the injured. He pushed two large basalt stones out of the way as they seemed to be doing nothing.

"I am not prepared to wait to toss that stone to the bottom of the deep. Let's do it while we feel good about it. Because that's the way it should be and you know it. Who has José?" he shouted.

There was a grand pause. Everyone looked around.

"I have him here and yes, you're right. It is the correct time," Francis said thrilled.

But it was quite difficult to tell what exactly was making him happy as he was continually touching Gem. The master of ceremonies walked over to Francis who was standing beside Eloïse. He thanked everyone for their sacrifices. Looking to Francis he said.

"Can I expect you to meet us at the main stage in ten minutes?"

"Yes, you can," he replied.

The Master of Ceremonies shouted, "Everyone shall witness this," as he walked off.

It was a little unnerving but you could understand. José had been a terrible menace and killed so many beautiful innocent creatures. Given the chance, he would have killed thousands more.

"Please sit beside me for a moment," Eloïse was looking up at Francis. "Firstly, your sister is fine. I explained why you did what you did to her. She was lost for a reason and extremely upset that it might be personal against her. But don't worry, she is fine. She needed to hear it from a different person! She understands and is looking forward to seeing you."

"Thank you, Eloïse." Francis was relieved.

"The other matter is to explain a couple of things to you. It's much like the conversation I had with your sister. You already know what I'm going to say Francis. You've only need to hear it from someone else. So listen for a moment, ok? The fact that you got so far was out of my control. Nothing was planned except for you to come in contact with Gem. That's it. The rest was your doing. Your mind made it feel you were both together a few months. What exactly happened between you two is for you, I know nothing. But from a person seeing you change from the outside let me tell you it was like a leap in evolution slowed down to a twenty minute movie," she explained.

"That's true. I can imagine what it must have looked like," Francis agreed.

"No matter. I watched a little and made my own interpretations. I hope you and Alex will stay friends, Francis. I didn't get any information from creatures on the beach about the situation. Occasionally I can see things happen."

"So you mean to say you don't know what I will do next?" he asked.

"Sorry Francis, I have no idea what will happen in ten minutes or five years. But I understood you enough to let you do what you wanted. There was no way I would have let you and your sister run riot on the beach. I trusted you. You're both intelligent and compassionate. I chose you because of the way you love. Like a child, unconditional to the end. By end I mean even you have limits. Like the feeling you're being used. Francis, I know you're old enough to understand that everyone is different, and at different stages in their lives. I had no control over the connection you established with Gem. The entire effort came from you and only you because that's the way you are. Another person would have produced a completely different outcome."

Francis lowered his head in silence. He wanted to explode because he knew she was right.

"There were others warning you about her or? I am guessing a few. You know something more about lust and love. You can't expect to understand it until you have experienced it. So believe me when I say that the first real love is nearly always friendship, nothing else."

"I've been in love before, Eloise," he answered.

"Yes, I am sure you have, Francis, but was it ever so easy? So nice."

"It was never so strange or intense. It was a nightmare."

"The strangeness made it different because it was coming from inside your head. You made it personal. I'm sure Herman told you Gem had been hurt many times and, to a point, she'd given up on the thought of finding a partner she could stay with. But that's hard considering the way she acts, believe me I know. It doesn't make her a bad person only a different person. You were picked because you both needed each other for a while. I nearly fainted when I discovered you went through a test with Sandstone. Honestly I was so worried you could have been hurt. In fact, I would love to know what you saw during that time. It sounds incredible!"

At this point, in his mind Francis was rubbing his head across Gem's perfectly shaped breasts lusting like a snake climbing a tree in the hunt for a bird's nest. They were so firm but soft to the touch. Cool, refreshing water was flowing over them and all he could do was drink; such was his thirst that when the water stopped he started licking them like a piece of chicken. Rolling it around in his pocket he pressed harder in some places as he rubbed with his fingers. Gentle but firm was his touch.

"Francis!! Francis!" Eloïse was demanding his attention.

"Sorry, I was thinking about it all," he said.

Eloise continued talking. Suddenly, Francis understood that she was unaware Gem was in his pocket. How could that be? It wasn't that he felt ungrateful to Eloïse for explaining her actions. He believed her but the situation had now changed, either for better or worse. It became more surreal when the music started playing in the background. Neva had thought easy going sounds might lighten up the mood a little. Nobody was dancing but the effect was starting to work. After what had happened that day, it was welcome.

The majority that could walk started towards the main stage. Many of the injured were being carried as they didn't want to miss the final act.

Smasher had again returned to Eloïse and Francis to report that he could not find Gem and had a number of creatures searching.

On hearing that, Francis felt kind of giddy. Here he was holding the one thing he shouldn't be holding but he couldn't let go as he understood the pleasure in having such an object. His mind started reaching out in thought. What was the possibility of getting new thoughts and feelings imprinted onto the stone; to get a different response from it. *Like another girl*, he thought. *Jesus Christ 'it's not you, it's the e talking.' Could that possibly work?* Sniggering as he remembered the words from that song by Soulwax.

It was similar to driving towards a traffic light as it turns red. If it's a large intersection, with no other vehicles around you would risk it and put the foot to the floor. But it wasn't a large crossing. It was a tight little thing he wanted to wrap around his neck and take home like a six-pack of beer. Nobody will know at home. I could get away with it for years.

"Perfect!" he said aloud. Francis wasn't thinking of Gem anymore. He was already dreaming of many other things that he might like this little piece of rhodonite to provide but its slight pinkness reminded him of those soft, dry lips. With all their cracks they were still perfect at turning him on.

Eloïse instructed Smasher to leave Herman where he was and she suggested that a small spell would keep him in place as the three of them walked away from The Cock Traven. By the time they reached the main stage there were thousands waiting to see the spectacle. A great cheer went up for Francis, Eloïse and Smasher, as they walked passed. They had delivered the final blows in the downfall of a killer. For the younger creatures on the beach, José was the name of a devil in old stories to scare children. Eloïse stopped at a distance from the stage.

"I am still quite weak. Please let me watch from here," she asked of Francis, while searching for a nice place to sit where the sand was not too disturbed by footprints.

Smasher planted himself down beside her but his weight caused him to sink into the sand. Francis tilted his head in agreement and proceeded alone to the stage. Walking up the steps felt like participating in the French revolution: Royalty walking to their deaths with peasants looking on. Turning his head and holding onto the side rail, he could see right back to the main stand being already above most of the creatures on the beach. At the top, he was greeted by the Master of Ceremonies and thanked again for everything he had done.

"Please let me show you the device."

To Francis it looked like any catapult you would have found on many castle walls in the middle ages. The main beam of wood was about twenty feet long with pulleys at both ends. It was in the firing position ready to use. Francis, like any young man, was excited by this war machine he faced and, for a moment, forgot he was about to send a creature to a terrible death.

José faced hundreds, maybe thousands, of years in possible darkness, alone with no chance of rescue. Like all the stones that enter the sea at such a depth, he could never return except by the natural laws of nature, or accidently being washed up onto the beach from a storm or plucked from the seabed by a scuba diver. With no means to use his powers it would be impossible and everyone knew this.

Francis was being shown the control panel, which looked quite fancy at first glance. The Master of Ceremonies was eager to explain that his cousin had spent three months making it to the design Herman had wished for. It was never intended to have a use at the games but it was felt tradition was lacking lately and the catapult needed to be a fully working machine.

Looking down there was a lever for the distance you wanted to toss an object. It started with a picture of a turtle meaning very slow. So you would expect the object would not go far, a middle button for a hedgehog which meant middle range, something like five hundred metres out to sea. The last was the image of a rabbit or hare. Being the fastest setting it was expected the object would reach nearly one mile. Francis pulled the lever into various positions and in doing so saw the working of the catapult in motion. Next to the lever was a single red button which was in the upright position.

Francis was asked to test the machine once with an empty bucket. The fluid motion of this contraption was amazing. On releasing the button, the main bar went turning in the opposite direction with the bucket raising nearly two stories high into the air. The power forced Francis to step back. It looked like the whole thing could fall apart. The stage moved with the setting at middle range and even the Master of Ceremonies and his aides were hanging on to the side rails.

The spectators cheered at the spectacle as the Master of Ceremonies quickly walked over and pulled the lever on the wooden consol. The strange noise of cogs, wheels and weights moving underneath their feet could be heard. The mechanism was resetting itself. Amazing, Francis thought. He had imagined it would have taken a lot of men to do that in such a short time. In less than a minute it was ready to fire again.

The crowd continued to cheer as the Master of Ceremonies went into a long speech regarding how better off the beach will be with this terrible crab gone for good.

Still holding Gem, Francis was listening to what appeared to be her voice. It was like a whisper forcing him to pay closer

attention as he felt he was missing what was being said. Was it
Gem talking? He had no idea. The problem was this incoherent
garble was so easy to listen to. No stress, no worries, perfect
comfort. As a child can enjoy in its mother's arms. Feelings
of love warmed his body. Encompassed by heat he appeared
content. He imagined it felt like being back inside the womb of
some goddess. *This is so sweet,* he thought.

He started swimming this vast ocean of beautiful colours
aware he was back where he started, that is at the very
beginning. Motionless he was drifting upside-down and wanted
for nothing. Was Gem trying to reset everything?

"Why would she want that, she hates me," he said to himself.

Francis was very confused and rubbed his face with his hand.
He was finding it extremely difficult to concentrate. Placing
Gem in his left hand, he pulled José out into the light. In doing
so he looked about the beautiful beach. The sea was very calm,
as if expecting to be tossed a sinner. There was nothing, not
a ripple to be seen to the horizon. He dropped José into the
bucket and looked towards the Master of Ceremonies. Francis
placed his finger just above the button.

"José, I don't know if you can hear me but you must know
that I understand you better than anyone in this world. I too
spent some time with her. We call it rhodonite in my language. It
contains the mineral manganese which gives it the pink colour.
The first reason I was attracted to her. After that, well, look
how you turned out man. I have nothing left to say."

He pressed the button and José went flying. Everyone was
screaming and jumping about. They went completely bonkers.
Nobody even heard the splash as he hit the water. He floated for
a moment, watched the sun's rays splash over the settling water,
then proceeded to sink into the deep, dark bottom.

The Master of Ceremonies meanwhile tried in vain to shout
over the cheering. It took a while for them to relax. When
they eventually did, the expression of relief on their faces was
wonderful to see. José was a rotten destructive creature whose
actions demanded his expulsion from the beach.

The Master of Ceremonies spoke and he was distracted by the noise of the catapult's mechanism working back into the firing position. Francis had pulled the reset lever and pushed the range to maximum.

Many creatures were asking what exactly is happening. There was suddenly major commotion on the stage. Smasher and Eloïse had stood up to get a better view but neither could be sure what exactly was occurring.

Francis and the Master of Ceremonies were having a fight. The situation quickly got out of control with a number of other creatures joining in. Everyone directly in front of the stage was passing information back into the greater audience. The rumor spread like wildfire, it was going to fire again. Eloïse started shaking as she understood what was happening.

"No!" she screamed with horror.

Smasher looked at her and instantly started running towards the stand. Francis couldn't understand whether he was angry, unhappy or delighted at seeing Gem in the bucket. He did however know he was doing his upmost to hide his true emotions. Looking at Gem, with his finger touching the button it went down all the way into its slot. Then, as he released his finger, gradually it stopped ejecting one third of its original height. A click registered that the button had been pressed in the first place.

"It's not the way I wanted to say goodbye, Gem, but you brought way too much baggage on this trip."

(TO BE CONTINUED)